JACK GANTOS

FROM NORVELT TO
NOWHERE

CORGI YEARLING

FROM NORVELT TO NOWHERE
A CORGI YEARLING BOOK 978 0 440 87031 9

Originally published in the United States by Farrar Straus Giroux Books
for Young Readers, 2013

Published in Great Britain by Corgi Yearling,
an imprint of Random House Children's Publishers UK
A Random House Group Company

This edition published 2013

1 3 5 7 9 10 8 6 4 2

The Random House Group Limited supports the Forest Stewardship Council®
(FSC®), the leading international forest-certification organisation. Our books
carrying the FSC label are printed on FSC®-certified paper. FSC is the only
forest-certification scheme supported by the leading environmental organisations,
including Greenpeace. Our paper procurement policy can be found at
www.randomhouse.co.uk/environment

MIX
Paper from
responsible sources
FSC® C016897

Set in Sabon

Corgi Yearling Books are published by Random House Children's Publishers UK,
61–63 Uxbridge Road, London W5 5SA

www.randomhousechildrens.co.uk
www.totallyrandombooks.co.uk
www.randomhouse.co.uk

Addresses for companies within The Random House Group Limited
can be found at: www.randomhouse.co.uk/offices.htm

THE RANDOM HOUSE GROUP Limited Reg. No. 954009

A CIP catalogue record for this book is available from the British Library.

Printed and bound in Great Britain by CPI Group (UK) Ltd, Croydon, CR0 4YY

For Anne and Mabel

Author's Note

The rural farming and coal-mining town of Norvelt is in the north-eastern corner of the United States. It was founded on socialist values of neighbor-helping-neighbor in 1934 and named for its founder, Eleanor Roosevelt, using the last syllables of her first and second names.

During the Great Depression of the 1930's Franklin Delano Roosevelt was voted in as President of the United States and Eleanor Roosevelt became the First Lady. She was very concerned about living conditions for out-of-work Americans and began a campaign to build towns for families that needed housing, work and social dignity, and thus she pioneered the Homestead Act which opened the door for the government to help create small towns for needy families. Eleanor was also the first wife of an

American President to hold her own press conferences, in which she spoke out for the rights of women and African Americans. In later life she served as the first chair of the UN Commission on Human Rights. The town of Norvelt has always been very proud to be named after such a great woman.

In *Dead End in Norvelt*, Jack, after errant gun play and a series of bloody nose disasters, is loaned by his mother to the elderly Miss Volker who was attempting to fulfill her 'duty to Mrs. Roosevelt' by writing history-laden obituaries for all of the original members of the town. But when the bodies of dead old ladies start to pile up with alarming speed, the police discovered that someone was murdering them with poisoned Girl Scout cookies. At first they suspected Miss Volker herself, but then Mr. Spizz – a man who was in love with Miss Volker – confessed that he had carried out the poisonings (or did he?). He then skipped town and hasn't been seen since.

But will the murders stop? Jack needs to remember his history lessons to avoid the mistakes of the past. Or will he be condemned to repeat them as he and Miss Volker hit the road in order to capture the killer in *From Norvelt to Nowhere*?

Jack Gantos

FROM NORVELT TO
NOWHERE

1

It was Halloween afternoon and I was swinging hand over hand like an escaped chimpanzee across the lattice of open attic rafters in Miss Volker's rickety wooden garage. She was circling directly below me and impatiently shouting out orders and crossly pointing up at what odds and ends of no-good junk she wanted me to inspect. I may have been acting like a giddy monkey in the rafters but I was really trying my best to help her out and even make her laugh, because this last while her old-lady moodiness was even more stormy than usual.

Mom had noticed too and just the other day remarked that Miss Volker seemed to be a shade more irritable since she no longer had her crusty old swain, Mr. Spizz, to kick around. He had kept bugging her about getting married, so she tricked him. She agreed to marry him but only if she was the last original Norvelt old lady alive. Miss Volker figured that would never happen and she could just keep him under her thumb forever. But suddenly a string of old ladies dropped over from eating Girl Scout cookies laced with deadly Compound 1080 vermin killer, and Miss Volker was the last old lady left. Spizz thought he'd outsmarted her, but before he could get her to the altar the police caught on to him. He confessed his guilt to Miss Volker, then stole her car and took off before he was captured. Since then nobody but the county police wanted to see him again.

"Spizz was a horrid man," Mom remarked, "but I guess it made her happy to have him to kick around. I just hope she doesn't go out and get a grouchy old dog to replace him."

"She won't be getting any kind of dog," I said while filling out my community service report for school. "She has me to growl at."

"I growl at you too," Mom added, and pushed my drooping hair out of my eyes, "but I love you, and I'm sure she feels the same."

I knew Miss Volker wasn't upset because of my attic antics, or even because of the criminal Mr. Spizz. She was irritable because of the nonstop radio and TV talk that was demanding an all-out war with Russia ever since we had caught the Russians hiding nuclear-tipped missiles in Cuba—and they were aimed at us! Last week, the president had come on TV and told the nation not to panic but to brace for the worst. War talk was turning into war hysteria.

Even the Norvelt newspaper got into the act. It published a letter from Mr. Huffer, the funeral director, who argued that we should "pull the trigger first, and blast the Russians back into the Stone Age."

Miss Volker was furious once she read that letter. Because the arthritis in her hands was especially bad that day, she had me dial Mr. Greene at the newspaper. I held the receiver up to her mouth as she gave him an earful. "You should know better than to print warmongering letters by the worst wagon-chaser in western Pennsylvania," she scolded. "Our founder, Eleanor Roosevelt, is dedicated to world peace at the United Nations and we should be too. If we pull the trigger first and start a war, the nuclear blasts and fallout will incinerate the human race and all evidence of its history. All the wild animals will drop in their tracks. Dead fish will cover the steaming oceans from shore to shore. Birds in the sky will wither and fall like October leaves. Even the nameless things that burrow deep in the dirt will find they've dug their own graves."

Mr. Greene apologized. Miss Volker hated war. She

was as angry as any bomb and wanted to blow war to smithereens.

And then, on the morning World War III was supposed to begin, the silver UFO-shaped gas tank behind the school cafeteria accidentally exploded. The propane fireball looked like a mushroom cloud over Norvelt. The explosion blasted a hole in the school kitchen and cracked a bunch of walls.

We were in class and terrified by the blast because our teacher had started the morning by pointing at the round Seth Thomas clock as it tick-tocked above the blackboard like a bomb. Casually, she had informed us that the Russian missiles launched from Cuba would begin "falling on Norvelt more or less around *noonish*. But for the moment, don't worry," she advised in a yawning, offhand way. "After we finish math we'll just take our sack lunches and a few board games and head down to the basement air-raid shelter, where the National Guard said we'd be safe."

"Safe as *cockroaches*!" Bunny Huffer had cried out derisively. She was the funeral director's daughter and my best friend, and about as short as a tall cockroach.

"Exactly," agreed our teacher. "Cockroaches will survive *anything*."

But the gas tank unexpectedly blew up before noon. In the classroom the overhead lights flickered and in an instant Bunny leaped up onto her desktop and hollered out, "Russian sneak attack! Run for your life!" Half of the class screamed and stampeded wildly toward the basement shelter, and the other half of us were paralyzed with fear while waiting for the searing white heat of a million nuclear suns to atomize our tears and eyes and brains and the rest of us into glowing space dust. I remember staring at my yellow pencil and thinking that it would soon look like a burning candle clutched in my sizzling hand.

However, nobody was hurt except for a few hysterical kids who were pushed from behind and fell headfirst down the concrete air-raid-shelter steps. The volunteer fire department whistle sounded and within minutes the Norvelt fire truck pulled up and doused part of the rear roof eaves, which had caught fire. While the firemen did their job out back the student body was evacuated through the front doors, and as we all stood on the baseball field our principal, Mr. Knox, announced that school was suspended.

We cheered loudly but he settled us right down when he shrewdly added, "Your time away from school will not be considered a holiday." We groaned, and as quickly as he could think it up he had given us homework. We were instructed to perform useful community service in "the generous spirit of our town's founder, Eleanor

Roosevelt. And upon your return to school I'll expect to see a written report of all you have done for Norvelt."

"But what about the nuclear war?" Bunny shouted out as she stepped forward to face him. As a group we all looked up into the air for incoming missiles but saw only a flock of extra-smart ducks heading north to Canada for cover.

"I have just received word," Mr. Knox replied cheerfully, "that the conflict in Cuba has been resolved for the moment. But nobody trusts the Russians, so keep listening to the radio for news."

"Do you mean to tell me that the war is called off?" Bunny cried out. *"Dang!"* She spit on the ground because she didn't dare spit on Mr. Knox. He had once played linebacker for the Pittsburgh Steelers and could probably eat a kindergartner for breakfast.

I knew Bunny was disappointed. She had told me her dad hoped for a war and had ordered a lot of expensive caskets for his funeral home. "Special *steel* caskets," she explained. "They are so *solid* you can actually use them for a personal bomb shelter. Plus, they have an adjustable air vent and a little blast-proof window on the cover where rescue teams can look in and see who survives, or not, without having to open the cover and find out the hard way." She pinched her nose closed and made a stinky face for emphasis.

Bunny was so thrilled about the idea of individual bomb shelters that I didn't dare point out to her that if there was a nuclear war you would actually be burying yourself alive.

So the reason I was monkeying around Miss Volker's garage attic during a school day was because Mom had started a Young Women's Club for Norvelt. Since every old lady in town, except for Miss Volker, had been wickedly poisoned and killed off by the escaped criminal, Mr. Spizz, Mom thought it was a good time for Norvelters to pitch in and donate their useless junk to raise money at a tag sale to help young women buy the dead-old-lady houses that were mysteriously vanishing.

Five houses had already disappeared, and all that was left behind of them were their garages, chicken coops, overgrown gardens, and water-filled foundations rimmed with snapped-off pipes and wires. Miss Volker said someone was stealing Mrs. Roosevelt's dream. She blamed the Hells Angels, who had bought her sister's old house, burned it down, then come back this fall to build a clubhouse on the ruins.

But my dad told me what was going on. To make extra money Mr. Huffer had been secretly buying the unoccupied houses and trucking them to a town in West Virginia where he resold them. Mr. Huffer denied doing this but Dad had been hired to drive the big truck that moved the houses, so I knew it was true.

It really bothered Mom that our town was disappearing, so she arranged for me to help Miss Volker gather her junk to sell.

"But why bother starting a club for young women?" I had remarked to my mother while eating breakfast. "We'll all be burnt toast in the nuclear war."

"Do as you're told," she replied, unfazed by my bleak news. "Somewhere in the world there is a war going on every day. The evil acts of others should not stop hopeful people like us from doing good deeds."

"Yeah, but this is a war of the whole world at once," I stressed, circling my arms above my head as if I were Atlas trying to keep the entire globe from exploding.

"For now," she said sharply, exasperated with my line of thinking, "our battle is to save our town, and without young women this town is just going to disappear."

"Hey, what about young men?" I asked, thumping myself on the chest.

"Women are the glue," she replied without hesitation. "If they run off, you don't have a town. Instead, you have a hobo village full of men who are as feral as wild dogs."

Maybe she was right, I thought. Where would Peter Pan and the Lost Boys be without Wendy to keep them from turning completely wild? And look at Dad when he didn't listen to Mom. After he had built his army surplus Piper Cub in our garage, he had dive-bombed people's houses. He flew above cars and dropped water balloons on them. He landed on the softball field during a game. He buzzed the hens at the community hatchery so many times they stopped laying eggs. He was having so much *wild-boy* fun people wanted him to leave town and get lost—and he did! He flew to Florida to find better work and he promised he'd be back to get me and Mom, but that hadn't happened yet. He was still off in Neverland.

I didn't want Norvelt to disappear, so when I finished my breakfast on Halloween morning I went down to Miss Volker's garage. It didn't take me long to say something that annoyed her. I was climbing a ladder up to the rafters when I asked what everyone in the whole world was asking. "Can America beat the Russians in a nuclear war?"

"Do they teach you *cause and effect* at school?" she hollered up at me. "Bombing them is like committing suicide. Even if they don't bomb us back we'll still die from our *own* fallout. There is no winner."

She was so touchy about the war. I flinched and knocked over a stained old ceramic pot that nearly beaned her. "Hey! Watch the *fallout*!" she growled. "I survived three wars and don't want to be killed by a bedpan and miss out on the joy of being evaporated by a nuclear blast."

"Sorry," I sang out. "But it's pretty cluttered up here."

Because the hooked fingers on her hands were curled up from arthritis, she had me use electrical tape to bind a small flashlight to her left wrist. She pointed the beam of light at things she wanted to donate. I used a rope to lower a rickety butter churn, an old ice cream maker, a Philco radio the size of a kid's tombstone, and a rusty Western Flyer bicycle with rotted balloon tires.

"I'm glad to be getting rid of this old rubbish," she said, and kicked out at the Philco radio. It didn't tip over and she gave it a foul-weather look. "I don't need this stuff, and it doesn't need me. Look at that butter churn for instance," she continued. "It's from my home-town of Rugby, Tennessee. I used it. My sister used it. Even Spizz used it. But now it's junk.

"In fact, now that I'm the last original Norvelter left I feel like a piece of old junk myself—maybe you can sell *me* off." She kicked the radio again, but it was a glancing blow off its rounded top.

"You are not junk," I countered, climbing higher into the rafters to reach for a dented brass tuba she had spotlighted.

"I'm useless here," she insisted, and this time she reared back and gave the Philco a swinging kick, as if she were kicking one of our new Hells Angels neighbors off her front porch. The Philco tottered on its weighted base but didn't tip over. She glared at it. "My pledge to Mrs. Roosevelt to be Norvelt's town nurse is fulfilled,

12

my duty is complete," she declared, "and now my twin sister in Florida needs an eye operation, so I may go take care of her for a while—perhaps for the winter. Who knows, maybe I'll find some old geezer down there and fall in love."

"Really?" I asked, and grabbed at the mouthpiece of the tuba. "Why fall in love?"

"You mean, *why fall in love at my age*?" she snapped back. "Does it surprise you that before the world ends this old lady desires someone to give her a big beautiful kiss?"

That is exactly what I meant and my cheeks began to throb and redden. "It was dense of me to say that," I added apologetically.

She shone the flashlight into my face. "Now, don't start blushing," she ordered, and sidestepped from beneath me. "If your Swiss cheese nose has a blowout again, I don't want you showering blood down onto my hair. I just had it done."

Her hair was as blue as a hydrangea and stood straight up on her head like the Bride of Frankenstein's. It was so stiff on the sides and so flat on top she could probably balance a bowl of goldfish up there.

"My nose has been fine since your last operation on it," I hollered back. "Totally under control. Not a drop in two months." I used to have nervous nosebleeds all the time, but ever since Miss Volker ran a red-hot veterinary tool up my nostrils and rotated it around real good, my scorched inner nose walls had healed into a solid dam of tough, rubbery scar tissue.

I had just tied off a rope around the tuba to lower it to the ground when Bunny Huffer dashed into the garage and yowled like a Tasmanian devil as she skidded to a dusty stop across the gravel. She startled me, and the rope slipped out of my fingers. The bulky tuba shot straight down like a hand cupping a fly. If the wide opening of that tuba landed directly over the top of Bunny's little head, it would swallow her up like a man-eating snake. She'd be squeezed inside the tuba like a corkscrew and no one in the whole world would have the lungs big enough to blow her back out.

But it landed with a dull note just in front of her foot. She looked up at me with a fearless scowl. "You don't want to flatten me," she warned, " 'cause I have some *incredible* news!"

"Another Russian sneak attack?" I asked.

"Better than *that*," she cried out.

"Well, don't just stand there looking like a yard gnome," Miss Volker snapped, referring to Bunny's stumpy size as she pointed the flashlight directly into her mousy eyes. "Spit it out before we donate *you* to the tag sale."

An impish smile slipped across Bunny's sweaty face

as if she knew what she was about to say would distress Miss Volker more than anyone in the town. She pulled her shoulders back and slanted her eyes to one side to avoid the interrogating beam of the flashlight.

"Well," she boldly announced with a flourish. "Private sources tell me that a certain very old lady named Mrs. Custer at house E-19 has returned to town. And you know what that means," she sang with a self-satisfied smile.

"Do tell me," Miss Volker replied with disdain. Her judgment of Bunny was soured by her vile opinion of Bunny's father, who smelled of funeral-home formaldehyde and bleach and enjoyed dead people a little too much.

"It means," Bunny explained slowly, calculating the impact of her point, "that you are no longer the last standing original old Norvelter in Norvelt."

Miss Volker's jaw slowly lowered like a flag falling to half-mast. "I was afraid Mrs. *Custard* might move back," Miss Volker said, with her voice carrying the heavy weight of her disappointment. "She called me last week from Utah and asked if it was safe enough to return after all the old-lady murders. I asked if she owned a pistol and she said yes, so I advised her to bring it with her and just shoot anyone who tried to poison her. I guess I should have made Norvelt sound more dangerous, but I thought all those old-lady murders in a row would keep her at bay." She sighed with regret as her shoulders slumped.

"Yikes," I said, "I don't think keeping a loaded gun in the house is a good idea for an old lady."

Instantly Miss Volker drew herself up and glared at me. "What is wrong with you?" she snapped. "First you don't want old ladies to be kissed. Now you don't want them to have guns. Honestly, without guns how do you think old ladies ever get kissed?"

Bunny saved me from a further tongue-lashing by butting in. "Well, she won't need to use the gun on herself," she suggested, "because she already looks half dead. I'm sure she'll soon drop over, which is okay with Dad because he could use the funeral business. He hasn't made a buck off a body since the last old lady hit the deck, and now this war is a *dud* for casket sales."

"What a vulture you are," Miss Volker remarked. "I bet this is the way you and your dad talk about me behind my back."

"No offense," Bunny said matter-of-factly. "We talk about everyone this way. Tailors look at people and know the size of their suits. Dad looks at people and knows the size of their coffins. It's just part of the funeral business. Every living person," she sang in a radio jingle voice, "is just a breath away from a payday for us.

"Anyway," Bunny carried on, changing the subject, "looks like Mrs. Custer returned to make her *last stand*."

"Good grief," Miss Volker cried out in frustration, and clawed at the air like a dog scratching a door. "Her name is Mrs. *Custard*. Not Custer! She may be the last *dessert* but not the last *stand*." Swiftly she spun around and gave the radio a solid kick. It held its ground.

I had read about General Custer and how he and his troops slaughtered Indians on the Montana plains until the Indians had had enough of it. At the Battle of the Little Bighorn the Indians turned the tables on General Custer and slaughtered the troops right down to the last man standing—and then they killed him too. I could imagine that bloody battle as if I were the last man killed and scalped and I felt a pressure build up in my nose kind of like when a steaming teakettle is just about to whistle. I thought for sure I was on the brink of my old bloody nose blasts, but after a moment the pressure retreated. The dam of scar tissue in my nose was still holding strong, and I dropped down from the lowest joist and landed next to Bunny.

"Oh, not to change the subject," Bunny said as she turned toward me, "but what are you wearing for trick-or-treating tonight?"

"The same as always," I replied, plucking cobwebs from my hair. "My Grim Reaper costume."

"Not that old thing," she burst out, and stomped her little foot.

"But I love my Grim Reaper outfit," I said, and struck a fearsome pose. "Everyone is afraid of the Messenger of Death knocking on their front door."

"You have to come up with something new," she demanded. "Something extra scary. Because I have something *killer* good, and I'm not telling you what it is just yet."

"Well, how about I make a Hells Angel costume," I suggested. "That's scary."

She made a blah face. "Come on," she encouraged. "Think! Make it one step scarier. Use your noodle."

I couldn't really think of anything scarier than the gang of Hells Angels that had moved into Norvelt like a nest of angry hornets.

"Okay," she said impatiently. "I'll give you a hint— *Gantos boy.*"

"Spizz!" I shouted merrily. "Yes. I could be Spizz." I turned and looked toward Miss Volker.

"That's psychopathic," she said, glaring at me and raising her leg back like a horse about to kick. "You should be ashamed to go as a menacing serial killer."

I should have been, but it sounded so deranged I knew it would be the best costume in town. And besides, Bunny was jumping up and down and waving her sausage arms as if she were on fire.

"Yes, Killer Spizz!" she hollered. "Poisoner Spizz! Murderer Spizz!" Bunny stood on her tiptoes and grabbed my shoulder. "And," she added, "I'll even loan you his adult *tricycle*. My dad bought it from the town and is planning to weld a passenger seat on the back and charge tourists a buck to ride it on a tour of the remaining dead-old-lady houses."

"That is shameful!" Miss Volker remarked. "This town is really going downhill fast."

I smiled at Bunny. "And now I know what you are wearing for Halloween," I said. She leaned forward and whispered in my ear.

"*Dead old lady*. But you better keep it to yourself because you-know-who won't like it."

"*Yep*," I whispered back, then shifted my eyes toward Miss Volker, who was still glaring at me.

"Bunny," she said harshly. "Take the wheelbarrow and haul this junk over to the Community Center. The two of you should be horsewhipped for making fun of dead old ladies."

Bunny grabbed the coiled body of the tuba and heaved it into the wheelbarrow as if it were a brass octopus. Then she lifted the handles of the wheelbarrow and buzzed off like a small outboard engine at the back end of a river barge.

Once she left, Miss Volker turned to me. "Death may seem a million miles away from you," she said with an icy voice, "but death has already reached my front porch and I don't need some peewee serial killer knocking on my door with murderous shrieks of 'Trick or treat!' "

She was always good at making me feel guilty about my morbid ideas. "Maybe I *should* be horsewhipped," I said contritely, and ambled toward her to gently inch the tape from around her wrist and flashlight without peeling off any papery old skin. I knew I should be sorry because there wasn't anything funny about what had happened to all the sweet old Norvelt ladies.

"Now that Mrs. Custard is back," I observed, trying to find something upbeat to say, "it means you aren't the last old lady alive in Norvelt, so Spizz can't marry you."

"That's good for me," she agreed without sounding agreeable. "But it could be bad for Mrs. Custard."

"What do you mean?"

"What if he comes back and does her in like he did all the others?" she suggested.

"He can't come back here," I said, shocked at the thought. "He'd be spotted."

"And they'd hang him," she said, and grotesquely stretched her neck over to one side and stuck out her tongue.

"That's awful," I remarked.

"Sure is," she agreed. "Because he deserves even worse."

"Worse than hanging?" I cried out.

"Way worse," she said coldly. "He deserves to have me tormenting him for all the days of his life."

Then she gave the Philco a ferocious kick from behind and it fell over onto its face. "Finally!" she proudly declared, and rubbed her hands together with the satisfaction of a job well done. "It took me a few tries but I put it six feet under for good."

2

When I returned home Mom was sharpening a kitchen knife against a whetstone and had a loose sack of purple beets to peel and slice. I could tell right away that she was peeved just by the deliberate way she set down the knife and stone and roughly wiped her hands on her apron. It wasn't the knife that worried me. When she was angry her eyes were sharper than any blade.

"I want to talk to you about something I found in your bedroom," she said seriously. "Something very important."

"Something mature?" I ventured to ask. "Or immature?"

"Immature!" she promptly confirmed, and in an instant picked up the knife and brought it down on a beet with so much force it split in two and shot both ways across the length of the countertop.

Oh cheeze, I thought as I followed her down the hall, what could she have found? There was a long list of taboo stuff hidden in my bedroom. If she'd found anything, I hoped it was just the dried-out roadkill squirrel I kept in my winter boot or the blacksnake skull I found by the garden.

My hoard of dead animal pieces was the least problematic of my secrets. If she discovered the BB gun Bunny Huffer gave me to shoot Hells Angels roaring loudly past my front yard, then I would be grounded for life. But I was too afraid to shoot at them, even though Bunny said it might lead to some good business for her dad. Also, I knew BBs would just bounce off their tough gray skin that looked like rhinoceros hide, and as I ran away they would track me down and then cut out my tongue and turn me into one of the fiendish tattooed baby doll mascots they barbwired onto the front of their Harleys.

So, instead of using the BB gun outside, I had made a secret BB gun target in my bedroom out of a big piece of cardboard. I drew a pretty lousy picture of a Nazi helmet sitting on a grinning skull. I had painted bull's-eyes inside the skull's eye sockets and they were now pocked and shiny with copper BBs from where I had shot them so many times. I knew if Mom found the BB gun and target, it would immediately remind her of me shooting Dad's sniper rifle at the drive-in on the first day of summer vacation and blowing myself off the picnic table and bursting all the capillaries in my nose and bleeding like a stuck pig. At that moment I wasn't sure who would hurt me the most: the Hells Angels or my own mom.

Please, I begged silently as I followed Mom down the hall, if you don't find the BB gun and target, I promise I'll bend the rifle barrel in a U-shape and just shoot myself in the chest.

But her temper was not scalding-hot because of anything I was worried about. It was something much worse.

She marched directly into my room and with a quick jerk of her hand lifted the corner of my mattress and slid it around to one side. What she revealed made me stiff with fear, and I struck a terrified pose like a plaster cast of one of those lava burn victims at Pompeii. She had found my banned stash of Classics Illustrated comic books.

"I thought I told you to read the *real* classics," she said sternly, and gave me a piercing look. "Especially now that school is shut down."

"These *are* the classics," I said reverently, and

reached toward them. "It says Classics on the cover—see? They're educational."

"Not comic book versions," she replied sharply. "I meant the whole original book." She pointed to a stack of dog-eared paperbacks she had pulled from the lending library shelf at the Community Center.

I knew what she meant. I wasn't stupid. I glanced at *Moby-Dick*. It was thicker than our old family Bible. Then there was *The Deerslayer*. *Pudd'nhead Wilson*. *The House of the Seven Gables*.

"The Classics Illustrated versions are just as good," I said lamely.

"No they are not," she shot back. "It's like saying being an immature boy is the same as being a grown man."

"But I'm a boy," I argued. "I should be doing immature boy things."

"And then you'll stay a boy forever. Believe me, I don't want to raise a big baby in this house. These," she said firmly as she pointed toward the real books, "are the kinds of classics you read as a boy and they mold you into a man. Those," she said with a sneer as she pointed toward the spread of Classics Illustrated, "are what cheaters and idiots read."

"But these books get me excited," I replied, defending myself.

"It's unfortunate that it takes so little," she said in a voice laden with scorn. She leaned over the bed and with both hands gathered up the comics as if they were a loose deck of filthy cards.

"You aren't going to ground me for this?" I asked meekly.

She cocked her head to one side and an amused smile drew up the corners of her mouth. "Reading these junky books must have turned you into a special kind of dumb boy," she said while with her knee she pushed the mattress back into place. "I wasn't even thinking about grounding you until *you* brought it up."

That was really stupid of me.

"No, I won't ground you," she continued, "but I'm just putting you on notice that if you do something this pathetic again, I will ground you."

"I don't want to be pushy," I said meekly, "but what are you going to do with my comics?"

"I'm going to make you take them down to the Community Center and donate them to the Norvelt tag sale—that's about all they are good for."

"Okay," I said glumly. When she left the room I looked through the stack. I still hadn't read my Classics Illustrated *Moby-Dick* and thought of hiding it, but I knew she would search my room after I left the house for Halloween, so it was better to do what she demanded.

I put on my baggy old-man work clothes to look like Spizz and slipped my comics collection into a bag with some Spizz costume props. As I sheepishly ventured outside onto the front steps Mom was lighting the Halloween candles in the carved pumpkins. She looked up at me and asked, "Where is your Grim Reaper costume? I bought you a new mask after you lost the last one."

I felt more than a little shifty inside. "I think I've outgrown that old costume," I said. "It's too young for me."

"Then what are you wearing?" she asked, and gave me a puzzled look.

After the comic book issue I really didn't want to tell her, but I didn't want to lie either. She despised liars more than comic books. So with a carefree wave of my hand I casually said, "Oh, I'm just going as silly old Mr. Spizz."

"Spizz!" she shot back, and stared up at me with such stunned disbelief she burned the tip of her finger on a match.

"Yeah," I said cheerfully, "Bunny thought it was a fun idea."

"Honey," she said right back, "you know Bunny has a dark imagination from working with her dad on dead bodies all the time, so her judgment may not be the best. Do you know what I mean?" she asked, wanting me to know *exactly* what she meant.

"I don't think it's a terrible idea," I said with a shrug, trying not to look her in the eyes. "After all, it's Halloween. I'm supposed to look scary so that ancient spirits and ghosts don't carry me away."

"I think you've already gotten carried away," she remarked. "It's in the worst taste possible to dress up as Mr. Spizz, given all the murders that man committed. But," she said, raising her hands palms out, "it is *your* choice what to wear or not—I'll leave it up to you because I think you are mature enough to make the proper decision."

Her stern face was like a stopwatch staring at me as the seconds ticked off while I struggled to make my "proper decision." Of course I knew she wanted me to change my mind and make a *mature* choice, but Bunny would kill me just so she could bury me in one of those bombproof caskets. Then I had a sharp idea.

"Well," I said in a very mature voice, "I had thought of going as a Russian nuclear missile but then figured the missile would be too scary for little kids, so I settled on the less distressing Spizz outfit."

"You do realize," she slowly warned me, as if she were crushing each of my false words under the heel of her shoe, "that bad choices lead to bad consequences."

"Bad choices don't matter anymore," I said flippantly. "Since we're all going to be blown up anyway."

Her eyes seemed to ignite with fury. "*Choice* is not about how we die," she said with contempt, "but about how we choose to *live*."

After that, what else could I do? I leaped off the top step and hit the ground running. "Don't worry," I said over my shoulder. "Nothing bad will happen. I promise."

"Your promise is what I fear most!" she hollered.

I broke out into a scary Spizz laugh as I ran across our dark yard and down the black hill. Halloween was a time to live it up!

Two minutes later I was the one mostly full of fear. When I entered the Community Center I went downstairs to the basement to drop off my comic-book collection. I passed by the old office Spizz had used when he worked for the Norvelt Association for the Public Good. He had a big title but was really just the town maintenance man. All day he rode his adult-sized tricycle around and gave tickets to people for not mowing their grass often enough or for not picking up rubbish on the street in front of their houses.

I noticed the door to his moldy old office was cracked open, and then I saw a flashlight beam sweeping the room. I kept my eyes on the door as I quietly tiptoed over to the table and set my classics down where donations were stacked.

I could feel my pulse pounding against the wall of

scar tissue in my nose. The police had not captured Mr. Spizz yet. Mr. Greene had printed a Crime Blotter notice in the *Norvelt News* that an "unknown source" reported Mr. Spizz had taken the train to New York City and was operating a mobile hot dog stand on a different corner each day. A week later, Mr. Greene printed a report that said Mr. Spizz was in Chicago and had applied for a janitorial job at a home for retired nuns. Every day there was a different rumor about where he was. But no one really knew for sure. He could be anywhere.

He could even be back in Norvelt, I thought, as I heard clumsy noises coming out of his office. Cabinet drawers were jerked open and things were being tossed about like someone was looking for something valuable in there. I got up some courage and edged toward the door when suddenly the flashlight was snapped off.

I didn't wait around to see who stepped out and I definitely wasn't going in. The place smelled like death and gave me the creeps, so I turned and took off. Anyway, it could have been anyone who worked at the Community Center. Maybe it was the new town custodian who took Spizz's old job. He was probably getting a putty knife and other special tools to scrape up all the sick-tasting Halloween candy and black licorice gum kids always spit on the church steps and jammed into people's door locks.

When I showed up on Bunny Huffer's front porch it was decorated with tall funeral-parlor candles and fake dead children in cardboard coffin boxes. One of the dead kids looked a little too much like me. There was even blood coming out of his nose. Bunny must have drawn the face because she was a good artist.

Twisted, I thought, and when I went to give it a pinch Bunny jumped out from behind a massive wreath of dried corncobs. I yelped and staggered back. She was dressed in an Indian costume with a feather headdress and a hard plastic hatchet with a sloppy line of fake blood on the edge.

"I ambushed you," she yelled in a voice that blasted out of her. "You are D-E-A-D!"

"What happened to the D-E-A-D old-lady costume?" I asked, gasping for air.

"My mom thought it was too mean," she replied unhappily. "But on the good side," she sang, reaching up to touch the stiff turkey feathers, "this headdress makes me look about twice as tall. I'm really tired of being so short, and when you dress up as a dead old lady you are as short as it gets—I mean, what could be shorter than being horizontal? Besides, even if the new lady's name is Mrs. Custard, I still like thinking of Custer's last stand, so the Indian costume works great."

"But now I'm stuck as Spizz the Killer," I complained. "We were supposed to go as a pair—a theme pair for 'Murder in Norvelt.' "

"Get over it," she said with a shrug. "Now bring your Girl Scout cookies and tin of 1080 and let's get you ready."

I really didn't have a tin of 1080 vermin poison in my brown paper bag. I had a Black Cat shoe-polish tin and I had painted a skull and crossbones on it with the numbers 1080. Instead of Girl Scout Thin Mints I had a wax-paper sleeve of Oreos.

We walked into the Employees Only area of the funeral parlor, where Bunny's mom and dad outfitted and applied face makeup on the cadavers before they posed them in the coffin for a public viewing.

Mrs. Huffer was modeling a nun's outfit in the mirror as if she were dressing up for Halloween. "Don't mind Mom," Bunny said once we hurried by her and slipped into a big storage room. "She's just making sure the blood is washed out of Sister Maria's habit before we send her back up to Seton Hill for burial."

Bunny opened a low cabinet door and lifted out a fishing-tackle box. When she opened it the rows of small trays folded outward like stair steps. "Your nose is too small and it swoops up," she said after carefully examining my face. "Spizz has a big potato nose." She reached into one of the trays and pulled out a wad of flesh-looking putty.

"What's that?" I asked.

"Cadaver wax," she said, working it in her hand until it took on the lumpy shape of a big nose. "It will stick to anything. It's really handy for plugging up holes in people after bad car accidents and facial gunshot wounds. Dad uses it all the time. Give him a photograph and he can rebuild a face for a close-to-perfect open-casket look. Now hold still."

I did and she pressed the wax nose hard against my own nose. "No bleeding," she ordered, and did some forceful pinching and final shaping until she was pleased with the outcome. "There," she remarked, "that is an authentic-looking Spizz honker."

"Great," I said, shaking off the nose pain.

"Do you want some yellow facial warts?" she asked, holding up a ribbon of glossy paper lined with gummy flesh dots. "Spizz had warts."

"Might as well," I agreed, and stuck my chin out as she pressed one on each side.

Then she snatched a pair of scissors out of the box. "Your hair needs a trim," she declared in a very determined way. "Spizz had a crew cut."

"Oh no," I protested. "I like my hair long."

"Don't worry," she said, coming at me with the open

33

scissors. "Even after you die your hair keeps growing. Now lean forward."

I did and she went to work on me. The hair fell like grass clippings to the floor. It didn't take her long, and when I ran my hand over my head I felt like I had become a little Spizz. It was disturbing. Then she took out a plastic bottle of powder and sprinkled it over my head and rubbed it in until what hair I had left was mostly gray.

"Wow," she said, pleased with her work. "You look just like him, only smaller—like his kid or something. It's freakish."

The thought of looking like Spizz Junior did not thrill me. And once Bunny and I started trick-or-treating we found out it did not thrill anyone else in Norvelt. After the first two houses we visited slammed their doors on us I turned to Bunny and said, "I think I should go home and change. Nobody likes my costume—in fact, they hate it."

"Don't be so thin-skinned," Bunny advised. "Ignore them."

"It's hard to ignore people who say, 'I'm going to call your mother and tell her how shameful you are.' Or 'You must take after your father because you think being cruel is funny.' "

"Okay, okay," Bunny agreed. "It's clear this town

has lost its sense of humor. You can't even crack a war joke without people going up in smoke. So let's go hit Mrs. Custard's house so I can do my Custer's last stand routine and you can go crying *wee-wee-wee-all-the-way-home* and change into your crummy old costume."

I agreed, but as we walked to house E-19 my every footstep seemed to take me down a bad path to something that was even worse. First, when we passed the Hells Angels clubhouse they were giving cans of beer out to little kids.

"Repeat after me," ordered a drunken Hells Angel dressed as a Viking warrior. "When I grow up I'm going to be a badass."

Bunny turned to go up their sidewalk.

"I'm a badass Indian," she hollered out, and waved her hatchet around. "And I want a beer or I'll scalp me a Viking!"

"You're too short to be a badass!" I growled, and yanked her away by her Indian braids.

"You're no fun," she griped as we moved on.

I picked up my pace because we were approaching a lot where the house had been jacked up and trucked away, leaving nothing behind but a sinister black hole of a basement. It looked like a mass grave big enough to hold everyone in Norvelt.

"Do you want to hide in there and scare kids?" she asked, and pointed at the sinister foundation.

"The only scared kid would be me," I replied. "Let's just go to Mrs. Custard's house and get this over with. I'm nervous enough as it is."

"Well don't start bleeding," she said. "Spizz didn't get nosebleeds and you'll ruin your disguise."

I reached up and touched my nose, but it was dry.

We quickly passed two more houses, then I took a deep breath and turned up Mrs. Custard's crooked path of mossy paving stones. The walk was lined with squat tubs of dead shrubs, and their dried-out branches clawed through our costumes like the twisted legs of upturned cats. The sagging thatch of several trees made a dark burrow of Mrs. Custard's walkway. I kept slipping on the stones and the skin across my knees and around my ankles felt shredded. I stooped over to scratch my wounds. The same fear that sent me running from the Community Center had me walking on my tiptoes like a spooked rabbit ready to bolt. By the time I reached Mrs. Custard's front door, and at the very moment my shaking fingertip grazed her bell, she suddenly yanked open the door.

"Boo," she said softly.

I let out a yelp and shot up into the air like an electrified spring. She yelped right back at me. That made me yelp a second time, because her face was shrunken inward like a rotten apple and when she yelped her false teeth jutted forward like a rack of small ribs.

But only her teeth were scary. When I landed on my feet I saw she was dressed just like a plump old lady in a pleated pink housedress, with fuzzy pink slippers and a pink sleeping cap that looked like swoopy strawberry icing. Her body was sort of cupcake-shaped and I thought maybe she was wearing a pastry costume.

"Hello, nice children of Norvelt," she said, greeting us so sweetly I felt even worse.

"Trick or treat," I said without much fanfare, and then stepped forward and went into my crude Spizz act. "Would you like a poisoned Girl Scout cookie?" I asked in a slobbery old-man voice, and offered her an Oreo.

"How kind of you," she replied, and that's when I noticed she was already holding a real Girl Scout Thin Mint in her other hand. She pointed to me with it and said with some amazement, "Not a moment ago a man gave me this cookie. He had a nose and warts just like yours and could have doubled as your grandfather. He rode up on a very large tricycle."

"Spizz!" I shouted as she raised the Thin Mint to her open mouth to take a bite. "He's back!"

"Don't eat that cookie!" Bunny cried out, and took a leaping swing at it with her hatchet. But she was too short and missed.

Startled, Mrs. Custard stepped back, popped the

Girl Scout cookie into her mouth, and crunched down on it.

"Spit it out!" Bunny and I yelled at once.

We must have scared her because she gasped and right away started to choke, but then with a determined dry gulp she sucked the cookie down.

"Spit it back up," I ordered, and held my candy bag open in front of her mouth. "Spit now! It's poison!"

"I'll just get a glass of water from the kitchen sink," she said, and swallowed roughly as she tried to clear her throat. "I don't want to spit up in front of you nice children."

Bunny raised her hatchet. "We aren't nice children," she cried out. "Now spit in the bag or I'll scalp you!"

Mrs. Custard leaned forward and reached for my bag but there was a sudden weakness in her legs, as if her bones were melting, and she dipped down a little at the knees like a curtsy before the queen. At that moment she looked directly into my eyes and I could see the sudden confusion in hers. Then she gagged and backed slowly down the hall like a troubled ghost retreating weakly into another world. She vanished through the open parlor doorway and a moment later only came back in sight within my mind when I heard her hit the floor with a solid thud and the windows rattled in their dry casings.

"Last stand," Bunny whispered, and snapped her fingers.

"Don't be cruel," I said harshly, scolding her in the same voice as I scolded myself. Then I shoved her forward. "Go help her up. Get her some water. I'll run and get Miss Volker."

It only took me a minute to cut through yards and reach Miss Volker's house. I pounded across the porch and ran inside shouting, "Miss Volker! Miss Volker! Mrs. Custard was poisoned by the return of Spizz and Bunny thinks she's had her last stand."

"That's not a very amusing Halloween story," Miss Volker growled out from the kitchen, where she had just finished loosening up her stiff hands in a hot pot of melted paraffin. "Be courteous toward the elderly."

"But I'm telling the truth," I replied desperately.

"The truth is most convincing when delivered with respect, young man. Remember that," she advised as she peeled the drying wax from her hands. "Tell me what's happened."

I took a deep breath and enunciated in my well-mannered movie voice: "Miss Volker, our dear neighbor Mrs. Custard has just seemingly been poisoned by a Girl Scout cookie we believe was given to her by Mr. Spizz, the 1080 murderer who is still on the loose, and now she has had her last stand and dropped to the floor and I'm guessing she may have ceased to live, but if she is alive and can be saved then she could use your help *now*!"

"God, you are long-winded," she remarked, and threw the last strip of wax into the hand-cooking pot as I grabbed her medical bag, which always sat at the ready next to the door. "You should be a politician. Now let's go."

Miss Volker was a brisk walker, but even if we had flown through the air on witches' broomsticks, there was nothing that could be done for Mrs. Custard.

When we arrived Mr. Huffer was already standing in the parlor with his black hat off in respect for the dead. He had covered her with a dark rubber sheet that resulted in Mrs. Custard looking like something suffocated under a collapsed trampoline. Bunny had called him on the house's telephone, and now we were all awkwardly standing around the crumpled sheet waiting for the police to arrive.

That's just when Miss Volker looked me up and down and realized the identity of my costume. "I thought you knew better than to dress as Mr. Spizz," she said sharply. "I should have the police arrest you for callous disregard of human life." Then she abruptly turned her sickened face away and refused to look at me.

I had already used up all my "I'm sorrys" for the

day, so I quietly parked myself in a corner like a junior criminal menace and picked off my warts and stuck them to the bottom of my shoe.

The police arrived and eventually asked me to explain what had happened a couple different times. I told them what I saw, but not how I felt. Then the volunteer ambulance pulled up with a doctor from Mount Pleasant and soon they were hauling poor Mrs. Custard out on a stretcher. When no one seemed to need me anymore I turned and began to walk back home.

On the way I passed the Community Center, which was always unlocked. I was so worked up I thought I'd go in and just borrow back one of the comics I hadn't read yet to later help me wind down and go to sleep.

I crept inside and quickly dashed downstairs to the donation table and chose my *Moby-Dick*. When I turned around I noticed a thin light shining out from the crack under Spizz's old office door. It chilled me to think that he had returned to poison Mrs. Custard, and if it was him in there now I had to do something. Even though I told myself to be brave I was still afraid of him. After all, he was a cold-blooded murderer, and adding my name to his long list of victims wouldn't bother him one little bit.

I grabbed a woman's clunky shoe from the donation table and threw it at his door.

The light didn't go off and I didn't hear any movement.

"Is someone in there?" I hollered. No answer. I knew the next thing I had to do was to open the door and stick my head in to take a look, but my hand would not reach for the knob. I was so terrified I just shrank down into a little baby version of myself and like a shameful coward crept silently up the basement steps and out the Community Center's entrance.

"You're willing . . . to scare an old lady . . . to death," I stuttered to myself as I tiptoed down the front stairs, "but you don't have the backbone to catch her killer."

I felt disgraceful and slunk away like a spineless shape. I lowered my head. A stone statue knew more about the darkness inside itself than I knew what was inside of me. I was alive, but nothing more.

I had just passed the unlit back corner of the building when I heard a twig snap and then something warm and bony clamped down on the back of my neck. I shrieked and twisted my head left and right but couldn't get away from the grip, which held me firmly like the talons of a hawk.

"*Gantos boy*," growled Miss Volker, mimicking Spizz's meat-grinder voice as she kept me hooked with her curled hand. "I'll see you down at my house in the morning. We have an obit to write up."

"Okay," I gasped, trying to catch my breath as she released her hold.

"And remember," she said severely, "when you go around scaring old ladies they will get you back."

"That costume was a real mistake," I admitted, then turned tail and trotted off.

I circled around to the rear of our house and entered through the back door as Mom passed out candy at the front of the house to some normal kid in a clown outfit.

I slipped into the bathroom to wash up. When I looked into the mirror that stupid Spizz nose was still stuck on my face, only it was smushed off to one side from my wrestling to get away from Miss Volker. I reached up to pull it off but then I paused. I knew better than to imitate Spizz. He was a murderer and a criminal— the lowest of the low—and it was disgraceful of me to sink lower than him.

I turned away and yanked off that ugly nose as if it were a big blood-sucking tick and I threw it into the trash can. I never wanted to see that Spizz nose again.

3

That night I read *Moby-Dick* and afterward I dreamed I bled a cask of blood from my nose. When I woke I expected to find my pillow had been wrestled into the shape of a soggy red whale. But it was solid white.

I hopped up and looked into the mirror but there was no red tide of blood foaming around my nose and trickling over my lips and chin. In *Moby-Dick* it was pretty gruesome to read how whales were tracked and harpooned until the windblown plumes of blood sprayed like flags of death from their red wounds. The whales died slowly and were hauled across the water to the mother ship and chained onto the side. Then they were gradually rotated so the blubber could be peeled from the flesh in one thick spiral, like peeling the coarse skin of an orange in a single strand. The crew axed the tough blubber into chunks and dropped the slippery pieces into cast-iron tubs and boiled them down into oil that was poured into casks and stored in the belly of the ship. The worthless carcass of the whale was then cut loose and a frenzy of sharks stripped the meat from the bones until the weight of the white skeleton slowly pulled what little sinew remained to the bottom of the ocean.

It was cruel how men could take the life of a mighty whale, which at one time could launch itself thirty feet above the churning surface of the ocean, and pitifully reduce it down to a minnow-sized flame that flickered in a bright dance from the spout of a small brass lamp. If only Aladdin could rub that lamp and wish the tiny flame back into a whale.

And I wished too that I could turn Mrs. Custard back into her old self, but no one could bring back the dead. I didn't kill her, but maybe she wouldn't have eaten that Girl Scout cookie, I agonized, if I hadn't dressed up as Spizz Junior. Maybe she would have thrown that poison Thin Mint in the trash instead of taking a bite out of it.

Then I imagined that Mrs. Custard could have given it to Bunny to eat, which was a dreadful picture to paint because then Bunny would have had her own "last stand" and landed on that toy hatchet. Or worse, Mrs. Custard might have given it to me and I might have saved it and later given it to my mother as a treat. That was a torturous thought, and that's another reason why all night long I had tossed and turned and dreamed like a harpooned whale gushing blood onto my pillow.

Perhaps Mrs. Custard would have eaten the cookie even if I hadn't dressed up like Spizz, but now I'd never know. Screaming out "Trick or treat!" on Halloween had always been so much fun. Now it would always seem like the shameful battle cry of a child assassin.

When I made up my bed I tried to put the dream of the bloody pillow out of my mind, but there was no masking what had happened at Mrs. Custard's house. And there was no hiding from wondering who I might have discovered at the Community Center if I had been brave enough to have kicked open Spizz's old office door when I heard the file drawers being slammed around. Maybe then I could have caught the killer in the act of sprinkling 1080 on that cookie before he delivered it. If I hadn't been such a coward and slunk away, nothing bad might have happened.

I was my own worst company, so I shuffled down the hall. Mom was weeding through her long cave of a closet for more old stuff to donate to the tag sale.

I leaned against the closet doorjamb and casually said, "I'm going down to Miss Volker's house to help with an obit."

"Oh, no. Who died?" she asked, and tossed some tangled wire hangers in my direction.

When Mom cleaned house she fell into a world of her own. Obviously, she hadn't heard the news yet. "A person who recently moved to town," I said nonchalantly. "I only saw her once and she didn't look too well." That wasn't the complete truth but it wasn't a complete lie either.

"That's awful," she remarked.

"It sure is," I replied.

"Well, return soon," she ordered. "I got a telegram from your father saying he was flying home this evening, and we need to spruce up for his return."

That got my attention. "Did the telegram say anything about us moving to Florida?" I asked, suddenly thinking that if I left Norvelt, maybe I could leave my shame behind.

"Not a word," she said with a grunt, and labored deeper into the closet as if hacking a trail through a jungle. "You know your father—he makes a mystery out of everything."

That was true, I thought. He kept the inner workings of his mind totally private. Mom and I could never tell if he had secretly worked out a brilliant master plan for our future, or if he simply made snap judgments when we asked him "What do we do next?"

"He also sent a package," she added, struggling to elbow her way to the very back of the closet.

"What's in it?" I asked.

"You'll have to wait," she said in a strained voice as she wrestled with mothballed coats that her parents would never have thrown away. "But believe me, it's a first for him."

"Did he send us an alligator?" I guessed.

"I don't want to spoil it for you—now run along so you can get back here and clean up before he lands in the backyard, or down the middle of the street, or wherever."

I got dressed, then hustled out the front door and down to Miss Volker's house. When I arrived I saw an official Norvelt violation ticket stuck to the outside of her porch door. I leaned forward and read it. Under VIOLATION was written: *You are the last old lady standing.* Under FINE it read: *One shotgun wedding!*

It was him! It had to be Spizz!

I ripped the ticket off the door and took it inside to Miss Volker. After I read it to her I could feel all the old-lady air in the room being sucked into her swelling lungs.

"Spizz," she uttered bitterly, as if his name were a

Transylvanian curse. "That thick-skulled white whale is going to get what he deserves," she vowed. "And it won't be a kiss on the lips."

"Should we call the police?" I asked.

She paused. "No," she said slyly. "They might catch him and just lock him up. I have a greater justice in mind for him."

"What kind of justice?" I ventured to ask. I remembered the Classics Illustrated version of *The Man in the Iron Mask* and thought thirty years with an iron mask locked onto your face could be a pretty good punishment.

"I believe I'm fated to put an end to him," she said firmly as she tried to bend her fingers as if she could strangle him. But her fingers were as stiff as rusty nails. "Lately my mind has been so full of turmoil over what to do with myself now that my Norvelt duties to Mrs. Roosevelt are done. I've been second-guessing myself for days. But now a great moment of clarity has saved me. I'm going to track down that thick-skulled white whale and then I'm going to *kill* him. I'll be his Captain Ahab."

"I've just been reading that story!" I cried.

And then I thought of something. "But didn't Moby Dick kill Captain Ahab?" I suggested delicately because she was so worked up.

"Not in my version," she replied with a sudden squall of emotion. "In *my* version I'm Mrs. Captain Ahab and I jam my ivory peg leg right down Moby Dick's blowhole." She stamped her foot down so hard I jumped back like a spooked cat. "Sometimes it takes a woman to get the job done properly."

She turned and gave me a severe look that squelched what I was about to say.

"Don't you *dare* feel bad for wanting to knock off Spizz," she commanded. "He deserves Old Testament justice—an eye for an eye and a tooth for a tooth."

"I just want to catch him," I said. "And give him to the police."

"And to think," she mused, "at one time I wanted him to catch me. I was actually flattered that Spizz wanted to be my swain—but no more. He's got to die! Yes," she said, commenting on what she had just announced, "my duty to Mrs. Roosevelt has one last chapter—and now my life has renewed purpose by vowing to end his."

I had never heard her talk that way. I must have looked stunned.

"Well," she asked, jabbing her fists onto her sharp hips, "would you like to remark on what I just declared? Or are you going to stand there with your mouth hanging open like the drop seat on a union suit?"

Finally I coaxed some words out of my mouth. "Miss Volker," I said, "this is not like you."

"You mean," she snapped back, "*I'm* not like *you*. You're a kid with a whole fresh life ahead of you. I'm an old lady who is close to the end of my life. If you kill Spizz, your life is ruined. If I kill him, my life is complete, and I won't care what they do to me."

"I'll care," I quickly replied.

"Then I would be honored if you would write my obituary someday," she suggested. "But for now it's time to write Mrs. Custard's obituary for tomorrow's paper. Please take your position."

I leaped at the opportunity to return to the old school desk in her living room. It was a lot easier for me to write about Mrs. Custard who was already dead than to talk about ways to send Mr. Spizz to the grave.

I lifted the hinged top of my desk and removed the pad of lined yellow paper and pencil I used over the summer when she had dictated the obituaries for each of the old-lady murders.

Miss Volker spread her ropy arms apart, and with her gnarled fingers balled up she stood in front of me as if she really was Mrs. Captain Ahab clutching the steering pins of a ship's wheel, while searching the seven seas for the white whale. The curtains were pulled aside so the light of the sun shone down on her. Then she cleared her throat and dug the heel of her old-lady shoe into the carpet like Ahab planting the tip of his ivory peg leg into a hole in the deck of the *Pequod*. She was my captain and I was her Ishmael.

"I'm ready to write, captain," I announced, as I lowered the desktop and raised my pencil.

"I didn't know her that well," she started, peering up through the windowpanes as if judging the angle of the sails. "But I do recall that Willa T. Custard came to Norvelt because of the Rural Electrification Act. In 1936 ninety percent of all electricity was in the cities and only ten percent in the country. The power companies did not want to pay the start-up cost of bringing electricity to the country dwellers. Instead, they wanted farmers to pay for the power poles, the power lines, the transformers, and all the labor costs of running electricity out to a farm.

"Very few farmers could ever afford that steep price. So President Roosevelt passed the Rural Electrification Act to help the poor farmers get electricity. The power companies protested and said it wasn't good for the government to help people too poor to pay for electricity. But the president was right and stood his ground against big business. The government hired large numbers of out-of-work people to carry poles and dig holes and erect the poles and run the lines and set the transformers and meters and wire the houses. And then, once more and more farms and country people got electricity, they bought electric water pumps so they wouldn't have the hard task of hand pumping water from a well. They bought refrigerators, and electric ranges, and water heaters so they could take hot showers and baths, and they even bought electric irons and vacuum cleaners and one of the most important items—the radio. People could then listen to news and music and plays and stories and jokes. And because life became a little easier they had more time to read books and play games and spend time with their families and friends, and suddenly the power companies saw their business grow and life for country people became fuller and richer.

"And we in Norvelt were made richer when Mrs. Custard and her husband, Henry Custard, both of whom worked on bringing electricity to Norvelt, decided to stay and join our community. After Mr. Custard passed away ten years ago, Mrs. Custard moved to Utah to be with her children, but recently she returned and now has been murdered in the same way so many Norvelt homestead ladies have been poisoned. Some people call it a mystery, but I do not. There is only one man who could have done this and his name is Edwin Spizz.

"Mrs. Custard was a great help to our country bringing electricity door-to-door, and we honor her for her service to the nation. But Mr. Spizz is a great criminal, and every criminal is a blight on the nation no matter if he steals candy from a store, or money from a piggy bank, or a bicycle, or a car, or a life. Every criminal poisons the health of the nation as if he were a secret agent working for a foreign enemy.

"In nature if you have corn worms in your cornfield, you don't call the police, you spray them. If you have beetles in your cabbage, you pinch their heads off. If you have mosquitoes in your ears, you swat them. Like pests, criminals destroy our great country from the inside out. Spizz is a blight on Norvelt and he shall be eradicated like any fungus or insect or worm that threatens the health of our fine town.

"As the last original Norvelter I pledge to you that Spizz shall find that the terrible swift harpoon of justice is in my hands."

She paused and I slowly dared to peek over at her because she was talking in a fearsome way I had never heard her talk before. "Is that all?" I asked with my pencil trembling above the notepad.

"What more do you want?" she barked back at me.

"Don't you always do a This Day In History piece to end the obit?" I said in a whisper. "Like with all the other old ladies."

"If you insist," she said reluctantly.

She threw her head back and marched in a wide circle beneath the ceiling fixture as if her face were the planet Earth orbiting the sun. The more she concentrated on what to say, and the more she circled, the more a dark shadow of wicked thoughts crept across her face until she was wearing the black mask of a total eclipse.

And then out of that merciless mood her mouth began to unwind the terrible oath of her vengeful thoughts.

"This day in history is like no other. Today is a mystery of history that hasn't yet happened," she stated. "But if history is a gun, then on this day the trigger has been pulled. Only time will tell us the day when the bullet strikes its target and history is made. Mark my words, I have a new purpose in life. I made sure this town was a pillar of health, but now I'll make sure Spizz is six feet under an unmarked stone."

I wrote it down just as she said it even though I wanted to change the words around because they sounded too harsh to me. She had taught me before that no one should practice revenge. But now her oath to bury Spizz seemed like an oath to bury her own beliefs.

"Is that good enough for you?" she asked, restraining her leftover anger.

"You're the captain," I snappily replied, and saluted.

"And don't forget it," she ordered. Then, as if her last blast of bitterness had ripped the sails that drove her anger, Miss Volker wilted down onto the couch and slouched over to one side, and soon I could hear her low snoring, which sounded more like the purring of a tired old cat.

She didn't move as I took my notes and typed them up on her clackity typewriter, and when I was finished I took the obituary down to Mr. Greene to print in the *Norvelt News*.

But after he read it he looked up at me with concern in his eyes and across his firm, even mouth. "I'm sorry," he said somberly. "But I can't print this. It's too severe. Besides, we don't know if it was Mr. Spizz who killed Mrs. Custard."

"But Mrs. Custard was killed with a poison Girl Scout cookie like a lot of the other old ladies," I stated. "Plus, whoever did it stole Mr. Spizz's adult tricycle from behind Mr. Huffer's house and that's how he got away. Who else would know to do something like that? Even a killer Hells Angel would be too embarrassed to escape on a *tricycle*. It has to be Spizz."

"It could have been anyone," replied Mr. Greene. "Besides, the police say they have a list of murder suspects to investigate, so I can't go around spreading rumors in the newspaper. That's not the Norvelt way. However, we did print that there is a reward for the capture and arrest of the killer—and that's a fact.

"Well, I know I didn't kill Mrs. Custard," I said meekly, "but maybe I scared her to death with my Spizz costume."

"That was poor judgment," he replied with a touch of disappointment. "But foolishness is not the same as murder."

"But everyone in town says it's Mr. Spizz," I argued, pleading my case.

"That could very well be true," Mr. Greene concluded. "But for now let's not rush to judgment. Go back and tell Miss Volker to revise her obituary. No one person can take the law into their own hands and be a vigilante, otherwise we'd have chaos, with everyone walking around with guns and shooting each other—and what kind of town would we have then? Certainly not an *Eleanor Roosevelt* town built on peace and equality."

He had made his point. "Okay," I said, and walked slowly back to Miss Volker's house.

When I explained to her that the police were tracking down other suspects and we had to rewrite the obituary she struck her salty pose. "Another suspect!" she cried out so fiercely the word split the air like an ax splitting wood. "That's like telling Captain Ahab that there were two white whales haunting the seven seas." She scoffed at the thought. "And by the time Greene wises up it might be too late for some other old lady."

"Like you?" I asked.

"Never. When it comes to me the white whale has a fatal flaw," she said sagely. "He loves me, and when he pulls alongside me for a kiss I'll return his love with a cold harpoon to the heart."

She decided not to revise the obituary, and by the time I returned home Mom was busy ironing all the clothes she was giving away and didn't hear me come in. When I entered my room I saw the open box Dad had mailed to us. It was empty, but my bed was laid out with a new outfit that Mom had arranged to look like a paper cut-out of a boy. I stood and looked at the flat outfit—flat shirt, flat pants, belt, socks, and shoes. I felt a little flat too. Steamrolled, I guessed.

4

Mom was flat in a different way. She was more of a paper doll princess. She entered my room holding a peacock-blue silk dress against her body as if it were a dance partner. "Look at what your father sent me," she said, gushing. "It doesn't look like anything you could ever find in Norvelt!" She spun in a circle and the dress fluttered around her like a shimmering butterfly.

"Go put it on," I said.

"Not until I take a bath," she replied. "After wrestling with all those smelly old clothes in my closet I don't want to ruin this." She smiled broadly and held it away from herself so she could look it up and down. "I'm sure it fits perfectly," she said happily, measuring it with her eyes.

"How did he know your size?" I asked.

"Honey," she said, like she could taste the word as she tilted her head to one side, "he's my husband. All he has to do is put his hand around my waist and he knows."

I had never heard her talk that way before. Something *had* changed.

She paused and bit down on her lip. "I have a secret," she said.

"What?"

"Well, your dad wants us to move to Florida and I'm beginning to think that it's a good idea. Especially after I heard more about this awful business with Mrs. Custard's death."

"True," I said, and lowered my head because I knew more about it than she did. "A lot seems to be changing around here."

"But one thing," she cautioned. "Don't tell your father that I told you I'm excited about making a go of it in Florida."

"Why? Wouldn't it make him happy to know you felt that way?"

"He needs to first make *me* feel happy," she replied, and gave her new dress a playful smile.

That smile could mean a million mysterious things, I thought. All I had to do to make her happy was to keep my room clean, follow orders, say "please" and "thank you," and every now and again sit on her lap and allow her to hug me and sniff the top of my head as if I were still her "sweet little baby boy."

"Your father may show up at any time," she said, suddenly sounding like my mother again. "Now take a quick shower and come back here and put on your new outfit so that we look perfectly put together for him. And don't use up all the hot water," she ordered, "because I need to take a bath."

"Don't worry," I said, grinning. "I *never* use up all the hot water."

I gathered some underclothes and headed down the hall to the bathroom. About two minutes later I was in the shower when Mom pounded on the door. "Hurry up," she called out excitedly. "He just phoned. He's gassing up at the airfield in Latrobe and will be here shortly. He said he's going to land on the roof!"

"I bet he can do it," I sputtered, and rinsed as fast as possible. Latrobe was only ten miles away. I turned off the water and wildly dried off by jumping up and down like a madman while giving myself fifty lashes with a damp towel. Then I stepped into my clean undershorts. I had just snapped the elastic around my waist when she burst into the room, and as if we were in a revolving door I was suddenly flung out into the hall and she was in the bathroom.

When I entered my bedroom I came to a standstill. I don't think I had ever gotten five pieces of new clothes at one time before. Even from the doorway they smelled wonderful, and when I stepped forward and touched them they felt so smooth and perfect. I put on the shirt and buttoned it up. Then I carefully put on the pants and the belt. I sat on the edge of the bed and slipped my feet into the socks and then worked each foot into the shoes. They were a perfect fit. In my dresser mirror I did look grown-up and mature. I put extra Vitalis in my hair because it was now so short. With a black plastic comb I carved a crisp part on the left side of my head and combed the uneven hair down to my ear. Then I combed the rest across the top of my head with one neat stroke and smoothed it down with my hand just as the barber taught me.

"You look like a college boy," Mom commented, startling me as she snatched a glance into my room on the way to her own.

I beamed. I felt transformed inside the new clothes and almost weightless because I was about to leap into the future without the heaviness of a past. I was so excited I just had to move around.

"Can I wait in the backyard?" I asked. "I want to be there when he lands on the roof."

"Yes," she said, "but don't make a mess of your

clothes. I don't want you getting all scuffed up before your father sees you looking so neat. No monkey business, understand?"

I did. I went outside and stared up into the sky but I didn't see him. I was eager to tell him the exciting news about the summer bomb shelter project he had me working on. The fall weather had been pretty warm, so last weekend I put in a few extra hours of digging the deep hole. That's when I made an incredible discovery. In a back corner of the hole I had unearthed the cover to an old bomb shelter that no one knew already existed. I hadn't opened it because I was going to wait for Dad to return home and share the discovery with him. I could just see him jumping up and down with excitement and slapping me on the back and saying "Good job, son" and bragging to everyone down at the Elks Club about what a great kid I was and that if King Tut's tomb hadn't already been discovered I would have been just the boy to find it.

I looked up into the blue sky and squinted. Where was he? I thought I saw him but it was just a circling hawk. To kill time I slowly walked along the airstrip he had built from the backyard on out through our garden and into the field behind the house. I made sure to walk softly because I didn't want to kick up any dust onto my new shoes and pant cuffs. I picked up a few loose stones that looked like Indian arrowheads, but they weren't and I tossed them aside. Where was he?

I was bored and started thinking about the bomb shelter. Wouldn't it be great, I thought, if I opened the lid and discovered that it was huge inside, like a land-locked submarine and fully stocked with beds and water and food and a generator for operating a ham radio so we could communicate with other bomb shelter families? And then I hoped it would be filled with books and magazines—maybe even a fresh pile of Classics Illustrated—and more new clothes. And then I thought that it would only take me a moment to open the bomb shelter cover and climb down and explore it by myself, and then I could put the cover back on and pretend like I didn't know what was in there and he and I could explore it together. I didn't see anything too wrong in doing that. I just had to make sure I didn't get my new clothes all dirty.

For a moment I thought I could dash into the house and get the BB gun and then pretend like I found it in the bomb shelter and that way I could keep it. But I didn't want to take a chance that Mom might catch me in the act so I canceled that thought.

I walked over to the hole I had dug and bent over and carefully rolled up my pants legs a few turns. Then I slowly inched down the slippery ramp of planks I had made for the wheelbarrow. I stood next to the bomb shelter cover, which looked like a round concrete manhole cover. I lifted the handle of my pickax and with the steel point of the pick tried to pry up the concrete cover from where it was snugly fitted into the top of the shelter. But the point kept slipping out and the cover wouldn't budge.

I figured it had been sitting there for a long time, maybe from World War I when people were afraid of gas attacks, not atom bombs. That got me even more excited because cool survival stuff from fifty years ago would be a great treasure. I picked up a sledgehammer and struck the cover a few times. I was in luck. The cover lifted just enough to where I could then jam the tip of the pick into the gap and lever up the edge. Once I got it going it slid off without too much effort.

Quickly I squatted down and tilted my head forward for a better view into the dark hole, but before I could make out anything specific the humid updraft of some smelly, putrefying flesh roared out of the hole like a raw fist. It hit me squarely in the face with a knockout punch. I stumbled back a step but didn't fall. What was that brutal smell? It was familiar but I was too stunned to think clearly.

I staggered around like a bowling pin about to tip over. Still, I kept warning myself, "Don't get dirty. Don't get dirty." My eyes glossed over and watered as I bent down to blindly feel around for the pickax. I needed to shift that concrete cover back in place before Dad arrived.

All I could think was that the flesh-rotting smell I was breathing into my lungs came from some sort of secret survival chemicals the people had stored in the bomb shelter to kill enemy invaders. It was probably homemade nerve gas that had leaked out and now I had breathed enough of it into my lungs to kill me. I didn't want to die, but I really didn't want it to also kill my dad. He had survived World War II and I didn't want him being killed by some leftover gas from World War I.

Despite my dizzy groping around I couldn't find the pickax to try to close the cover.

"Stay clean," I kept muttering. "Don't get dirty. Don't panic. You can do it."

I took a deep breath to calm myself, but the smell was so potent I pinched my nostrils shut with one hand. That helped a little and with the back of my other hand I kept rubbing my burning eyes in order to clear up my watery vision, and that's when I saw that instead of tears I was crying red blood out of my eyes and wiping it on my sleeve.

"Ohhh, cheeze-us-crust!" I wailed. "The blood is *back*! And it's leaking out my *eyes*."

Stay calm, I said to myself. Think this through. I figured my nose must have started bleeding, but because I had it pinched tightly the blood backed up and was now pushing out of my eye sockets.

"This is so bad," I whimpered. I felt my legs giving out as I sobbed bloody tears. "I'm dying," I moaned hopelessly. "I've been gassed to death."

There were sparkling stars and meteors diving in circles behind my eyes. And then everything around me became edged in gray, and then it got darker and darker.

That's when I lost it. I blacked out on my feet. I must not have fallen down right away. I must have first stumbled around stiff-legged like the living-dead and circled about the hole groaning and twitching and chewing on my lips as blood sprayed out from the rims of my eyes. My arms stuck straight out from my sides like a scarecrow. I had no idea how quickly or slowly I was dying, but my numb legs could just barely hold me upright as I inched forward in nervous spasms, and then I shockingly hopped like a frog right into the middle of the bomb shelter opening.

It was the sudden splash and slap of mucky water on my face that snapped me out of my stupor, along with the incredibly sharp pain on the underside of my outstretched arms where they hit the solid concrete rim of the round opening. That hurt, but thank goodness my arms were sticking straight out or I would have been fully submerged in the smelliest rotten-flesh stench ever.

"Oh, cheeze-us-crust!" I shouted again, and regained some of my senses. And then my brain began to function. "This isn't nerve gas!" I cried out. "The bomb shelter is filled with a whole town full of rotten, mushy dead people!"

I think it was right then that my nose burst open like a blown-out tire and I got a little hysterical because I was bleeding foamy blood out of both my nose and my eyes. I stuck one finger in an ear and pulled it out to check for blood, because Bunny Huffer said that a lot of dead people bleed from the ears from brain melt. There was no blood on my fingertip, so I was momentarily relieved.

Suddenly I remembered Mom's warning about not getting dirty. "My clothes!" I gasped, horrified by the mess I had made of them.

I don't know how I did it but I shot up out of that hole like a swamp rocket and stumbled rabidly toward the house like a snapping, gasping, dangerous animal.

"Mom!" I hollered toward the back door. "I fell into a bomb shelter full of toxic human remains."

In an instant she rushed out onto the porch, then froze. I didn't know it at the time but the horrified look on her face was caused by what she smelled and not from what I had just told her. "Don't get near me," she ordered, because I was muddy and dripping with blood and brown muck and staggering unevenly toward her and she was all made-up in her beautiful new dress.

"I need help," I begged in a pathetic baby voice. "Help me, *Mommy*!"

"Stand back!" she commanded as if she were leveling a shotgun at me.

I took a step forward.

"I'm warning you!" she said sternly, and then her nose flared open and immediately flattened against her face like a door slamming. "Whatever you fell into," she said, "they are not the kind of human remains you are thinking of." She quickly pressed the palm of her hand against her flattened nose in order to keep it in place. "You must have cracked open the septic tank cover and you fell into your *own* human remains."

"I don't know what you mean," I cried, running in place in my sloshy shoes because I would have collapsed if I stopped moving. "My *own* remains? Tell me quick because I think I'm dying."

"When you flush the toilet where do you think it goes?" she asked, and removed her hand from her face.

I thought about it. "A hole in the ground?" I guessed.

"What a genius," she groaned. "And that *hole* would be called a septic tank, and that is where all the human waste from this house goes."

I must have looked stumped. I was thinking that a

septic *tank* was some kind of military vehicle with a cannon mounted on the top.

"I mean *poop*!" she shouted impatiently.

I held the back of my hand under my nose and sniffed myself. "Cheeze-us-crust!" I howled, and began to shrink slowly down inside the thick brown crust of my disgusting clothes. All I could think of was poor Mrs. Custard hitting the floor with a final thud, and in a moment I would be right behind her. Then I looked back toward my mother. "What do I do?" I begged, and extended both arms toward her. "I'm still your sweet little baby boy."

Her reply was like the swift lash of a whip. "Get the garden hose," she snapped, and pointed toward the side of the garage where it was coiled.

I ran toward it, and when I turned it on the first thing I did was blast myself in the eyes with ice-cold well water until I could feel them floating in their sockets like shivering guppies.

A moment later I felt Mom grab the back collar of my shirt and hold me up. She had quickly taken her dress off and now was standing in her full slip and sheer stockings.

"Dear God," she said in her church voice, "if you spare him from any horrid disease, I'll devote my life to doing good deeds for others."

"Me too," I said.

"Don't open your mouth," she ordered. "The germs will rot your stomach." She began to roughly unbutton my shirt and arm by arm pull me out of it. Then she worked my shoes off and threw them over her shoulder. Then she wrestled my pants down to the ankles, and leg after leg tugged them off my feet and flung them to one side. "Your new never-been-worn-before clothes are ruined," she declared with disgust. "They smell like some baby's nasty bottom."

"How was I to know the bomb shelter was a septic tank?" I said, trying to defend myself even while thinking I had become one gigantic skid mark.

"Anyone with a brain," she replied, "would know that you don't jump into a hole that smells like the elephant cage at the zoo!"

And that is when I first heard Dad's plane circling around just above the treetops. He must have been pretty stumped up there looking down at us as Mom tried to yank off my streaky brown underwear while I pranced around until I finally broke away from her grip and dashed witlessly toward the house. And he really must have been puzzled as to why Mom was wearing soaking-wet underclothes and looking like someone had dragged her through the mud. But no matter what he guessed about us he would have definitely known something was wrong when even from his cockpit he could see her swirl around and point toward the back door as she roared out over the noise of his engine in the voice of an angry lioness, "You are *grounded*!"

Maybe that's just when he dropped into a dive and swooped down over the house and yard and tossed a huge bouquet of yellow roses out the window. They almost hit her, but she wasn't upset one bit. She picked them up and buried her nose into the thick carpet of rose petals as if they were an oxygen mask.

He circled around until I could hear him pull back on the throttle as he lined up the wheels with the dirt runway we'd made where our cornfield used to be.

He touched down as Mom blew him a kiss and I slip-slopped down the cellar steps toward the basement bathroom. What could possibly go wrong next? I thought.

Then, with some little relief, I thought that nothing could go wrong next. The worst was over. Surely, it had to be over. And I was now alone, which made my shame and embarrassment almost tolerable.

So it was pretty surprising that while I stood naked under the longest scalding-hot shower of my life my mother yanked back the curtain and looked me up and down as if I was a threat to the health of all the citizens of Norvelt and even the nation. She was wearing a bleached-white one-piece bathing suit that made her look like a no-nonsense nurse from a Swiss sanatorium. Her face was set for combat. In one rubber-gloved hand she held a homemade bar of acidic lye soap she used for laundry, and in the other gloved hand she had a stiff horsehair brush she used for scrubbing out the toughest grime and stains in Dad's work clothes.

"I'm naked," I sort of squeaked out. "I'm too old for this."

"Move over," she ordered, stepping into the shower like a boxer stepping into a ring while I quickly tried to adjust my posture in order to hide my private parts. "When I'm finished with you," she said sternly, "you'll still be naked but you'll also be antiseptic." And then she lathered the soap onto the brush and proceeded, one harsh stroke after the next, to remove a layer of skin from every square inch of my body.

When I finally rinsed away the lye soap my scorched skin felt hotter than the water. I stepped out of the shower, and as I reached for a towel she pulled it away from me. "Drip dry," she commanded. "Shimmy like a wet dog." After a minute of spastic gyrations I was positioned in front of the medicine chest mirror, where I watched her shave off what top hair Bunny had left behind until my skull was as blinding as the lightbulb hanging by its neck from the ceiling.

"Stand with your arms and legs apart!" she barked like a policewoman. I did, and she leaned toward me and with her nose about an inch away from my body she sniffed me up and down each arm and leg and the whole middle of my body and even inside my ears. Then, as she slowly sniffed her way across my upper lip, she suddenly inhaled even harder, as if she were vacuuming the unhealthy air from my lungs right up through my nostrils. She didn't like what she smelled. Something was wrong. Her nose crinkled up and she opened the medicine chest and removed a Q-tip. Then she uncorked a bottle of rubbing alcohol and poured it on the Q-tip and slowly twirled it up my nose. I couldn't breathe, but I didn't dare make a peep because I was trying not to think where she might next stick the head of that Q-tip.

5

How could I have known as I stood there naked and embarrassed in front of my mother that falling into that septic tank of human waste would turn out to be some kind of fairy-tale baptism that transformed me from a kid who could do nothing right into the mature young man Mom hoped I'd become?

It only took a week before I was standing at the kitchen sink and properly washing the dinner dishes. When the telephone rang I wiped my hands on a towel, and when I picked up the receiver the opportunity to prove my new maturity to my mother was on the other end.

It was Miss Volker. She didn't sound right. Her voice was quivering so much her chattering teeth seemed to type the words she spoke. "Do you know what day this is?" she stammered.

"Do you mean what is This Day In History?" I replied. "Or do you need to know that this is November 7, 1962?"

"I *mean* did you listen to the evening news on the radio?" she asked. And before I could answer she abruptly added, "Today we are living in *history*. Today is the day that Eleanor Roosevelt passed away."

I paused and so did she, and while she wept for a minute I quietly waited. This was not a day in history Miss Volker ever had on her calendar. She had written about war and peace, heroes and villains, and the rich and the poor. Day after day her calendar of history marched forward with new facts and faces. Now the sad news of Mrs. Roosevelt's passing would be added to this procession of time, but for Miss Volker I knew she would feel it every day of her life. Once she blew her nose and took a deep breath I thought she might have pulled herself around, so I ventured to say, "I'll be right over to help with the obituary."

"I'm not ready," she replied, sniffing. "I need to settle down and give some thought as to what I want to say. I'm a scrambled mess at the moment."

"Then let me know when you want me to help," I offered. "I'll do anything you need. Anything. You name it."

"Well, I do have one little favor," she ventured to request, with some mystery in her voice as she perked up a bit, "but let me speak to your mother. I'll need her permission for what I have in mind."

I called Mom to the kitchen and passed the phone over, and as she listened to Miss Volker she nodded her head and repeated "Yes, and yes, and yes to that too" about a dozen times, and by the end of the week I wasn't sitting in school, or working on one of Dad's dig-till-you-jump-into-a-septic-tank projects, or helping Mom organize yet another community event. Instead, my mother had loaned me out to Miss Volker to be her dependable, all-purpose traveling companion on the train to Hyde Park, New York, where Eleanor Roosevelt was now buried next to her husband, President Franklin Roosevelt.

"Do everything she requires of you," Mom said strictly as she stood in front of my dresser drawers and began to set aside clothes I would need for the forthcoming trip. "And do everything by the book. No cutting corners. No drifting off into outer space when you should be planning ahead on how to help her up or down stairs, or with her hands—remember, she can be helpless." Mom sounded just like Dad and, like him, she was never finished with giving orders. "Her concerns come first and yours come second, if at all. That is what a mature boy does—he *serves*."

"You mean like a *servant*?" I asked, not enthused by the job description.

"No, like a good, loyal friend," she replied with her jaw firmly set.

"And I'm to do everything she wants?" I asked. "If she says 'Go jump in a lake,' then I jump in a lake, right?"

"Without hesitation," Mom replied, showing some impatience with my attitude. "She's brokenhearted at the moment, and it's up to you to provide her with a steady hand and keep her on an even keel. Her whole life was about *serving* Eleanor Roosevelt. I can't imagine what she might do next, but she's a great friend and for now we have to help her get through this rough patch."

She was right. Miss Volker had treated me like her best friend. I think she was sixty-five years older than me, but it sort of evened out because I was her youngest friend and she was my oldest friend. I made her feel younger and she made me feel older. I asked questions and she gave answers. I made her feel smart and she made me feel clueless. She was helpless and I was good help.

We were a perfectly mismatched match, and five days later I carried our small suitcases onto the late-night train in Greensburg. The weather had turned cold and it was starting to spit snow. As the engine whistle sounded we rolled forward and I pressed my face to the window. The snow was picking up. Mom spotted me. I waved and she blew me a kiss. Then, just like in a romantic movie, we grew farther and farther apart and the only thing that kept us together was our love for each other.

Miss Volker and I settled into our seats. She quietly opened a book and I opened an egg sandwich Mom had made me for breakfast but I knew it would taste better for dinner because it was still warm. I'd ridden the train before on visits to see some family in Altoona, but this was my first big train ride across the whole state. In the dark, there wasn't much to see out the windows except for sweeping car lights on a distant road, or a neon restaurant sign. When Miss Volker reclined in her seat and closed her book I reclined too and closed my eyes. I slept almost the whole way, with Miss Volker snoring next to me, and when we arrived at Pennsylvania Station in New York the next day it was like we had time-traveled from a sleepy old Pennsylvania full of tidy farms and barns to a new wide-eyed Pennsylvania jam-packed with bustling people inside the most gigantic building I had ever seen. The entire city of New York might have been under that roof for all I knew. I wanted to drag my feet and look around and explore the station, but Miss Volker was on the move.

"Keep up," she said sharply when I drifted toward

the ringing chimes and flashing neon flippers of a pin-ball parlor.

I carried our bags and stayed a step behind her. We left the train station and went outside. People passed by me wrapped in heavy coats with hats pulled down and their frosty breaths trailing behind them like chimney smoke. We caught a taxi to another train station across town. On the way we drove through Times Square, and I frantically looked around at the subway station entrance for a tiny statue of a cricket because our teacher had read us *The Cricket in Times Square*, which we all loved. I was going to tell Miss Volker about the book, but when I turned toward her she looked deep in thought, and so I didn't bother her with any cricket-sized questions. I spotted a hot dog stand and looked for Mr. Spizz, but it was run by a young guy wearing a New York Yankees jacket.

At Grand Central Terminal I kept looking up at the amazing domed ceiling that was brightly painted to look like the stars at night, and I set down my suitcase and reached up toward them as if I were standing on the very tip of the North Pole. I kept trying to make eye contact with Miss Volker because I wanted to ask about everything, but she kept her eyes front and center and her jaw as tight as a locked drawer.

Then suddenly she froze in midstep. "Stop!" she ordered. "Do you feel that?"

"What?" I asked, staring down at the ground as if I was searching for loose change.

"The vibrations," she said delicately, and tapped the tip of her shoe on the terrazzo floor.

I stood still and could feel the floor shaking.

"Deep below the floor where you can't see," she explained, "is where President Roosevelt and Eleanor had a secret train tunnel for their special Pullman car, the Ferdinand Magellan, named after the great explorer. During the war the car was bombproofed and renamed U.S. Car No. 1. The Roosevelts used the secret tunnel to avoid the crowds. The train stopped at a private elevator that took them directly up to the Waldorf Astoria hotel."

"Wow," I said. "Can we explore downstairs and try to find it?"

She looked toward the lighted face of the clock. "We have a train connection to make. Hurry up."

I grabbed the luggage and we leaned forward and dashed off down a corridor toward a platform. In a few minutes we caught a local train to Hyde Park station. The train route took us north, with the tracks sometimes teetering just a few feet from the snowy banks of the Hudson River. I looked out the frosty window and wondered what ever happened to Henry Hudson after his crew rebelled and set him off his ship in Hudson Bay. I turned to ask Miss Volker if she knew more about the famous explorer, but her chin was down and her eyes were wet, so as Mom advised I kept my question to myself and just waited to be told what to do.

When we arrived at Hyde Park and stepped off the train we found the station platform was still tented in yards of coal-black bunting from the funeral procession. President Lincoln's funeral train had passed through Hyde Park Station. President Roosevelt's U.S. Car No. 1 had stopped here. Now it was as if our own train had traveled the distance between the stations of Tragedy and Sorrow.

Miss Volker fit right in, draped in her long black dress, black woolen coat, and black knit hat. Even the long lines of grief in her downcast face seemed to be etched in jet-black ink. I looked like her "hired hand" in my mismatched brown tweed suit and homemade plaid tie as I carried our scuffed-up leather suitcases. I kept my eyes lowered as we solemnly marched down a black carpet that was so thick our shoes were respectfully hushed.

But once we entered the station waiting room the scene shifted again and a more pleasant mood erased the cloudy gloom of the platform. We stood facing a cheerfully painted wall showing peaceful colonial life on the Hudson River. There were lines of stout sheep and cows all posed on their hind legs as if ready to dance. Stripe-shirted boaters rowed along the banks of the river and cheerful picnickers spread out under summer willow trees, and in the middle of this peaceable kingdom hung a large portrait of Eleanor Roosevelt entirely edged with wreaths of sunny yellow roses sent from dignitaries around the globe.

"The whole world knows yellow roses are her favorite," Miss Volker said, stepping through the dark wreath of her own grief as she stood smiling in front of the portrait.

"They are Mom's favorite too," I remarked.

"Smart mother," Miss Volker said, then she leaned forward and kissed the portrait of Mrs. Roosevelt on the cheek. That single kiss didn't satisfy the size of Miss Volker's love, so she pursed her lips and kissed the portrait on the other cheek.

I was smiling a little too much when she turned and scowled at me. I shrugged. "What?" I said innocently. "I've never kissed a picture before—it's kind of funny."

"Then you've never lost a parent, or a best friend, or a good pet, or a sainted lady named Eleanor," she replied, and drew her shoulders up.

I thought about that for a moment. "I did kiss myself in the mirror once," I admitted.

"Now *that* is abnormal!" she declared with a smile. "Only a narcissist would do something that perverse."

I wasn't sure if a narcissist was a person who loved

himself too much, or was like Siamese twins who kissed each other. I was a little confused but I did make her smile, and that was a break in the clouds.

I wasn't sure I had another joke in me and was relieved when a taxi driver wearing a blaze-orange hunting cap opened the station door and hollered out, "Anybody need a lift?"

"We do," I called back. He stepped forward and picked up our suitcases, and I steadily held Miss Volker's arm as we followed him to his car, which he had left running to keep it toasty warm inside.

Once we arrived at Springwood, the Roosevelt home, I paid the driver from the wad of travel money I was in charge of. Miss Volker began to confirm our return ride to the train station, so I hopped out and carried our small leather suitcases into the gift shop and checked them with a uniformed guard who set them on a luggage rack. Then I trotted back to the taxi. Miss Volker had finished talking to the driver, and as the car pulled away I escorted her into the gift shop.

I took a deep breath and remembered what Mom had said as she packed my suitcase for my overnight stay in a New York hotel. "You have to take care of her. Be the grown boy—no, be the young man both your father and I expect you to be."

I wanted to be that boy who could be counted on to

act like a man. And now Miss Volker and I were here and there was nothing left to do but bravely do what we had come to do. It was time. I turned and looked Miss Volker in the eye.

"Are you ready?" I asked in a steady voice, and firmly reached for her elbow. She nodded, and together we stepped out of the back door of the gift shop and cautiously shuffled along an icy sidewalk of fresh snow that was peppered with coal ash and grit.

Perhaps because of the cold weather there were no other visitors that I could see. We took it slow and easy, and when we reached the arched passage through the thick gray wall of cypress trees we came to a stop. Before us spread the orderly winter garden with its pruned beds of silent roses where Mr. and Mrs. Roosevelt were buried. Miss Volker's hands felt like those dormant roses turned inward against the cold, and I hoped the warmth in her heart, like the roses, would return for a spring season.

In the center of the garden a green mat of fake grass had blown away from where it had covered Mrs. Roosevelt's fresh grave. The exposed scar of yellowish dirt glinted like frosty nuggets of gold heaved up under the lowering western sun.

When Miss Volker nudged me with her elbow we started forward again. I thought of all the people who, three days ago, had just walked where I was walking. I might have been stepping where President Kennedy had been, and Miss Volker might have been walking in Jacqueline Kennedy's footsteps. President Truman had been here and President Eisenhower. I was walking where they had been, and they had been here for the same reason Miss Volker was here—to say goodbye to the greatest American lady they had ever known.

When we approached a low hedge at the gravesite, more coal ash had been thickly scattered on the viewing area so people wouldn't slip. Since we were the only people in the garden we stood as close to the gravestone as we could reach. There were several inches of pure white snow piled on the top of the low hedge and across the wide shoulders of the stone. We stood there a long time without talking. I figured Miss Volker must be having a conversation with her memory of Mrs. Roosevelt. It was a very lengthy conversation.

After a while my feet became numb, and inside of my too-tight church shoes I flexed my toes like a cat curling his paws. I rocked back and forth from toe to heel. I slowly lifted and lowered my legs. Beneath my soles ice cracked in thin glassy chips. I wiggled my fingers inside my wool gloves.

All along I kept peeking up at Miss Volker's bowed face for any sign that she was ready to leave, but her face was as carved and hard as the solid ROOSEVELT headstone she stared at. Her ungloved fingers were now steepled together in prayer. I knew it had to hurt for her hands to be exposed to the cold, but I didn't want to interrupt her by offering my gloves. This was her one moment to show Mrs. Roosevelt a lifetime of respect.

Earlier I had taken my hat off as my mother had taught me to do when I entered a graveyard, but my ears ached with cold and my stubby hair gave me no warmth. My brain felt like a bubble of air trapped in a cube of ice, so I put the hat back on and pulled it down over my ears as far as I could.

"Please, Mrs. Roosevelt," I whispered to myself, "I know you are dead, but let Miss Volker wrap up her chat with your spirit before I'm forever frozen like some freakish kid gargoyle at your gravesite."

Miss Volker looked down at the watch on her wrist, then glanced toward the opening in the cypress trees where we had entered the rose garden. "Okay," she said. "I'm ready."

"Ready to leave?" I asked with relief, and clutched her elbow.

"No, ready to write the obituary for the *Norvelt News*," she said with renewed strength, and elbowed my hand away as if I were a pickpocket.

"I don't have a pencil or paper," I replied. "I'm not prepared."

"Open my purse," she instructed. "It's all in there. I knew if I came here I'd get inspired."

I opened the purse and removed a ballpoint pen and a notebook. At the same moment I got an unexpected jolt when I saw a hefty silver revolver in the bottom of her purse. Oh cheeze, I thought, but it wasn't the right time to ask why she had a revolver on the trip unless she might use it on the train to get some old guy to kiss her. She must have had a better reason than that but my brain was too frozen to think.

I closed the purse and gripped the pen as if I were holding an icicle. I could barely say "Go," as my jaw was rusty with cold. I lowered the tip of the pen against the paper as Miss Volker grandly threw her head back, straightened her shoulders, and with her right hand pointed directly at Eleanor Roosevelt's name.

"She was born," Miss Volker started, "on October 11, 1884. Yes, she was born into a rich family but her wealth did not spare her from family tragedy. Her mother died when she was eight, and her father died a year and a half later. She was sent off to England to be educated like a proper lady and later returned to New York, where she married the future president, Franklin Delano Roosevelt. She had six children, one of whom sadly died as an infant. When her husband moved to

Washington in 1913 as the assistant secretary of the navy, Eleanor joined him. This was the beginning of a powerful new world for her. Living in Washington opened her eyes, and she began to realize her greatest wealth was her opportunity to make positive changes in America. Not only did she raise her children and help nurse her husband through polio, but she worked for the right of women to vote, helped form trade unions to protect women and men on the job, and started a factory to help disabled people find meaningful work. She taught history courses at a school for girls, she wrote for newspapers, and she edited a magazine.

"At the worst point of the Depression, once her husband became president, Mrs. Roosevelt increased her efforts to improve the lives of all Americans. She looked beyond the barricade of grand monuments that surrounded Washington and found before her a broken nation where so many were suffering through poverty and hunger. She rolled up her sleeves and got busy, and to our good fortune she started the little town of Norvelt, where she nurtured us with homes and education and jobs and the belief that farmers and coal miners were as important as presidents and generals. She did so much for so many, but she knew she was only one person and could only do so much on her own. So in the end she worked for the United Nations, with a goal to make every nation understand that each living soul around the world has more in common with each other than not, and that the true wealth of the world is not power, but peace and equality for all.

"I thank her for the riches she brought into my life. She gave me purpose of work and dignity in helping others, and through her efforts she certainly changed my life, and the lives of every Norvelter for the better."

"And their kids too," I chimed in. I wanted to thank her for more but decided to avoid saying anything about septic tanks and instead added, "Thanks for giving us a good school." I didn't mention anything about the blown-up walls because that wasn't her fault.

"Amen to that," Miss Volker said, and I think she patted me on my head but I couldn't tell because my entire head felt as numb as a massive tooth that was about to be extracted. I was frozen, and even with the warmth of my closed hand the ink in the pen began to solidify and skip and then it stopped and I thought my blood would stop flowing too.

"The pen is frozen," I said to her. "Can we finish later?"

She swung her gaze toward the gap in the cypress hedge, and then back down at her watch. "We can," she agreed. "But for now let us sing Eleanor's favorite hymn." She cleared her icy throat.

I couldn't sing because I didn't know the words, but

it didn't matter because my throat was a frosty tunnel and if I took a deep breath my lungs would be glazed in a cocoon of ice.

"O Lord," she sang in her wavering voice, "make me an instrument of your peace."

She paused to catch her breath for the next line and that's when our cab driver reappeared, dashing through the gap in the cypress hedge. He ran up the sidewalk calling out, "Hey, lady! Hey, lady!" as he waved a black-and-yellow envelope over his head. I looked up at her and she smiled.

"Perfect timing," she said under her breath.

"Perfect for what?" I asked, but there was no time for an answer.

About twenty feet away from us he suddenly slipped on a patch of ice and one foot shot straight up into the air as if he were an acrobatic circus clown. He bent over backward and I expected a disaster, but in a split second he reached behind himself with his free hand and stopped his fall. Still, he continued to glide toward us balanced on one foot while his back hand steered him along the ice as if it were a rudder.

"Lady," he panted as he slowed to a stop and sprang forward onto both feet. His steamy breath, like tufts of white cotton, seemed pulled out of his mouth as if he were a pillow being unstuffed.

Miss Volker whispered a hasty "Rest in peace," before she slowly turned her rigid face toward him. "May I help you?" she asked.

"The Western Union office called our dispatcher," he wheezed dramatically, "and asked me to deliver a telegram to you. Whoever sent it knew you would be out here." The envelope trembled in his hand as if a frightened idea were trapped inside.

I took the envelope, but before I read it the driver must have read my mind.

"I'll wait for you in my cab," he said, rubbing his roughed-up hand on the side of his wool slacks.

"Yes," I agreed, and he walked away less dramatically than when he arrived.

"Jack," Miss Volker instructed, "please open it. I am afraid it is bad news."

My freezing hands were nearly as stiff and useless as hers as I clumsily ripped the envelope unevenly down the side. Maybe it was bad news from my mother, I thought as I removed the message and struggled to unfold the paper.

"Read it," she begged, exasperated with the fumbling pace of my hands just as she always was with her own. I finally unfolded the telegram, but when I looked at it I couldn't read it.

"These words don't make sense," I said. "The letters are mixed up."

"Just read it phonetically," she insisted. "I'll translate it for us."

"Via multe amis fratino," I read, struggling with the words.

"That's Esperanto," she clarified. "The international language of peace. My father taught it to us."

I didn't know what Esperanto was but continued anyway. "Mortis je la okulo doktoro. Venu al Florido nunj. Faros funebra planoj antau ol vi alvenos. Sincerely, Mr. Hap."

She narrowed her eyes at the telegram and jerked her head away from it at the same time, as if it was giving off a malicious smell.

"What is it?" I asked.

"This is very hard for me to say," she replied in a steely voice as cold as the air. "My sister has died."

"Your sister died?" I asked, shocked and trying to get a clear sense of what had happened. "The one getting an eye operation?"

"Something terrible must have gone wrong," she guessed. "And I have a sixth sense that tells me Spizz is behind this."

"Wait! Before jumping to conclusions," I said, sounding *exactly* like Mr. Greene, "let's think this through."

"He killed Mrs. Custard," she replied, "and now he somehow got to my sister as a way to break my heart."

"We don't know that," I argued.

"One murder leads to another," she pronounced. "Think *that* through." Then she raised her contorted fist over her head and growled up at the leaden sky. "You hear me, white whale!" she shouted bitterly, and stomped the hard pathway like Captain Ahab striking the deck of his ship. "You are a *dead* man!"

I don't know if Spizz heard her but a security guard making the rounds did. He stared across the rose garden and I did exactly what my father would do. I pointed at the side of my head and spun my finger around. "Cra-zee," I silently pantomimed. He nodded and walked on. If she had caught me at that moment, she would have pulled out that big silver pistol and shot me.

"Well," she said, suddenly invigorated and turning her attention toward me. "Do you have anything to say about all of this?"

I would normally have pointed out that she seemed more angry at Spizz than sad that her sister had died, but once again I thought I should hold my tongue and be the mature boy my mother had expected of me.

"I think we should go back inside and warm up," I suggested.

"Right," she agreed. "We have plans to make."

"What kind of plans?" I asked.

"Whale-sized plans," she replied.

The pathway was still icy, so she lowered her head and leaned on me for balance as we slowly shuffled back over the ash-blacked walkway to the gift shop inside the house. Once there, she took a seat in a wooden side chair with her head cradled within her open hands.

"Are you okay?" I asked after a few minutes, because I didn't know what else to say. It was the dullest question to ask, but I was afraid to mention her sister because she might start hollering about killing Spizz again.

"I'm thawing out," she replied. "And the more I thaw the more ashamed I am of myself. Look at me, I've really failed to live up to Mrs. Roosevelt's example. She devoted her life to peace and I've become a cranky old lady intent on violence."

"It's just a bad moment," I said.

"It's not a bad moment that is likely to pass quickly," she replied. "Ahab lost his leg and every leg has a twin, and now I've lost my twin. Every time I look in the mirror I see her face. If I don't get Spizz, I'll be too ashamed to ever look into a mirror again."

"But Spizz isn't an eye doctor," I said, attempting to talk sensibly. "He couldn't have anything to do with this."

"But he has an eye for evil deeds," she replied darkly. "And I will see to it that his deeds are the rope that hang him from the highest yardarm."

I took off my wool scarf, which was warm from my neck, and wrapped it around her hands. "Just rest," I said. "You'll feel better." After that, not another word was spoken as she pressed her face into the scarf, and I figured she needed a private moment.

I hadn't eaten anything since we hurriedly grabbed some sandwiches and drinks before catching the train at Grand Central Terminal in New York. When I saw the candy rack at the souvenir booth I drifted over and bought a 3 Musketeers bar. It was too sweet, but to let time pass I allowed each soft bite to slowly melt in my mouth as I picked through a spinning rack of postcards. When I finished I threw away the wrapper and bought a postcard of the rose garden in bloom with an inset photo of Fala, the president's favorite dog, who was buried close to his side. I paid for a stamp and mailed it to Mom. Miss Volker had gone to the ladies' room, where she must have freshened up, for when she returned she had a smart look in her eyes, rouge on her cheeks, and a solid plan on her mind.

First, she had me call my mom on the gift shop's phone. I called collect, and when Mom answered I had to shout over the operator's voice "This is an emergency!" so Mom would accept the charges. Then I told her that Miss Volker's sister had suddenly died and there was a change in our travel schedule. Mom listened and summed up the situation. "There is no other choice but to stick with her and continue to do any and everything she needs."

"Okay," I said. "That means it's okay to miss school and everything else, right?"

"I'll tell Miss Volker to tutor you along the way. I'm sure she knows something about everything. And," she added rapidly, "your father has flown back to Florida and is chasing work around in that flying coffin of his. When he checks in with me I'll tell him you're headed for Miami. Maybe he can be in touch with the sister's husband and meet you there and help out. So call me collect every chance you get. If you hear me tell the operator that I'm not home, just know I'm okay and have nothing new to tell you. If you have something important to say to me, blurt it out like you just did and I'll tell the operator I'll pay for the call."

"Okay," I said to all her instructions. "Count on me."

"I am," she said. "And Miss Volker is counting on you too, so keep an eye on her. When people are stressed they do odd things—and when they are old they do *really* odd things."

"Odd like what?" I asked, and for a split second pictured the big silver pistol in her purse.

"I can't say for sure but you'll know it when you see it," she said. "So stay sharp. Old people can be erratic, and very cunning."

Next, Miss Volker called her brother-in-law, Mr. Hap, and quickly went over a few details, including inviting smelly Mr. Huffer down to prepare the body for shipping back to Norvelt. And just like that the taxi driver returned us to the Hyde Park train platform and we backtracked to Grand Central, then took a taxi to Penn Station. We booked sleeper car tickets on the next day's East Coast Champion train to Miami, where we planned to meet up with Mr. Hap. Then we exited Penn Station and stood on the noisy curb and watched the traffic rush by.

"Look out for crazy New York drivers," Miss Volker warned me, swiveling her head back and forth like an old owl. "One of them hit Eleanor Roosevelt a couple years ago when she was crossing the street. It didn't kill her, but it was the beginning of her end."

"Do you want me to add that to the obituary?" I asked.

She thought about it for a moment. "I don't know," she said. "Then we'd have to add that one time she fell asleep while driving and injured a bunch of people and knocked her own front teeth out."

"Are we writing an obituary or a biography?" I asked, but before she could answer, the light changed and we dashed across to the Hotel Pennsylvania.

That night, when I crawled into bed I thought I knew exactly what our plans were for the next week, but I had no idea that I was the most clueless kid in the world.

6

I was flat on my back and lazily stretched out across my private roomette bunk on the East Coast Champion train and my parents were hundreds of miles away.

After a long layover in Philadelphia to take on freight we were under way again. Every thirty-nine feet the train wheels steadily clacked across a steel joint that connected one rail to the next, to the next, to the next—all the way down the zigzag spine of the Atlantic coast. Outside, the heavy wet snow was pelting against the window and sticking. We had slowed down a lot but it didn't bother me. Mile by mile the cold was falling farther and farther behind me. Miss Volker had told me Washington, D.C., was our next big stop, with sunny Florida just a few days beyond. When I stepped off the train, I figured, there would be nothing left of the snow but a puddle.

I yawned. As I settled my head into my folded-over pillow the hypnotic clacking of the wheels was like a small hammer tacking my eyes shut.

I was trying to stay awake and finish reading the new *Dr. Jekyll and Mr. Hyde* comic book I had bought at a newsstand in Penn Station in New York just before Miss Volker and I boarded the train. She had sent me to find if any magazines had extended obituaries of Eleanor Roosevelt but I was too late. They were all bought up.

However, as I looked around I spotted a display rack that was loaded with a new comic book, *The Incredible Hulk*, which looked weird, but the newsstand owner said it was based on *The Strange Case of Dr. Jekyll and Mr. Hyde*. He had a stack of that old story in a Classics Illustrated edition.

"What Mom doesn't know won't hurt her" is what Dad always said, so I bought a copy of *Dr. Jekyll and Mr. Hyde*. Then I went running from newsstand to newsstand until I had a huge stack of Classics Illustrated titles. I figured by the time I got to Florida and then back to Norvelt I could just leave them on the train for some other kid to read. After all, *sharing* was a classic Norvelt way of life.

Dr. Jekyll and Mr. Hyde was a fantastic bloody story

of good versus evil, but with a twist. Instead of two conflicting armies going after each other in combat, or two vengeful fighters going toe-to-toe in a boxing ring, the good and evil were equally split up and slugging it out within the same person. The battle raging within Dr. Jekyll was tearing him apart. His evil equal, Mr. Hyde, was dead set on destroying him.

Still, no matter how gripping the story was, and how much I pondered over what good and bad stuff was within me, the constant clacking of the metal wheels slowly lulled me into a droopy-eyed trance. I gradually lowered the comic book onto my chest and slipped into a deep, black velvety sleep like one of Mr. Hyde's murder victims who would never again see the light of day.

I don't know how much time had passed after I fell asleep when suddenly there was a loud *thump-thump-thump* on my door. I pushed the comic to one side and quickly took the single step from my narrow bunk to the roomette door and pressed my eye against the tiny glass peephole.

I was hoping it wasn't the suspicious ferret-faced man I had seen staring at me with his pinched eyes and his nose pointing at me like an accusing finger as Miss Volker and I ate a snack in the rear observation car. That long, thin nose of his kept rotating toward the far door like the magnetic needle on a compass, but I wasn't going anywhere in his direction.

Luckily, it wasn't him thumping on my door. Nor was it the ancient sleeper-car attendant returning my only pair of shoes. When I boarded the train in New York he noticed the leather was caked with grit and coal ash from Hyde Park. He was so insistent that he take them to his workshop for a good cleaning that I untied and stepped out of them. I hadn't seen him since. Instead, the eyeball staring back at me through the magnified peephole may have belonged to the evil-eyed Mr. Hyde, because on the other side of the hole a fiery red pupil glared menacingly at me as if it were my own demented split personality that was planning to take over my bunk.

"Who's there?" I asked timidly.

In response there was a cracking, head-high bash against the door followed by Miss Volker's sharp, impatient voice. "I know you are in there," she cawed. "Because I can see that squirrelly brown beady eye of yours, and the confused mind behind it!"

I jerked my eye back and blinked. It was true that I had squirrelly eyes. "Suspicious eyes," my mother called them. She should know, because I was always up to something she didn't approve of, like reading illustrated versions of great classic literature when I should have been reading the *real* book.

"Now open up!" Miss Volker demanded. "Or I'll splinter this flimsy cardboard door in half like Moby-Dick ramming the *Pequod*."

103

I pressed my eye back against the peephole. "If you are Miss Volker, then answer me this," I asked, wanting to show off my *Moby-Dick* knowledge from reading my Classics Illustrated edition. "Why did Melville name the ship the *Pequod*?"

"Because the *Pequot* Indians were all brutally killed off by the Puritans," she replied. "And the pure white whale was avenging those black sins of the Puritans."

"A-plus!" I exclaimed.

"Now open this door before I harpoon you with a hairpin right through your beady eyeball," she threatened. She painfully clenched her stiff, quivering fingers together and removed the long thin hairpin from the ropy braid coiled on her head so I could see she wasn't fooling. "Now open up!"

I slid aside the brass dead bolt and yanked the wooden door wide open just as the train careened around a tight bend and leaned sharply in my direction. Miss Volker had been in the act of once more hammering her anvil-heavy head against the door, and when the train tilted she gave out a squawk and lunged toward me as if she had pitched herself off a precipice. I held out my arms to catch her, but she came at me like a howling wildcat and I stumbled back onto my bunk as she mashed down on top of me. I was just quick enough to twist my face to one side so she didn't slam her jutting chin into my nose. Instead, she crushed my ear into something that must have looked like a wrinkly slice of dried apple.

"A half hour ago," she reminded me, with her steamy breath making my ear hole damp, "I told you to meet me in the observation car. What's taking you so long?"

"I went but you weren't there," I replied, straining to get the words out. "And that creepy ferret-faced man from earlier was there again so I came back here."

"Well, that's good to stay away from him," she said. "I think he's a detective. When I called Mr. Huffer about my sister yesterday he told me to look out for private detectives."

"Why?" I asked, shocked that a detective was after me. "Am I in trouble? Did my mother hire a detective to keep an eye on what I was reading?"

"No, but she should have. Huffer told me he figures those old ladies bought a lot of no-good life insurance from someone they *trusted*—but the insurance company didn't have to pay out if the old ladies died because of a criminal act—which they did. The families are so angry about not getting any death benefit they put the 'dead or alive' reward out on Spizz. Now every private detective on the east coast is trying to catch Spizz and cash in on the reward."

"It doesn't make sense that Spizz would be on this

train," I reasoned. "Why would he show up here if he just killed your sister in Florida?"

"Maybe the detective thinks I'm next on Spizz's hit list," she speculated. "He does have a love-hate relationship with me."

"Well, even if Spizz showed up, that scrawny ferret-faced guy couldn't arrest Spizz," I said. "Spizz is old, but he's big. He'd throw that guy off the train."

"I doubt there is only one detective. They always travel in pairs," she said knowingly. "There is an obvious one and a sneaky one. We've seen the obvious one, but I haven't spotted the other one."

"He'll be the muscle," I figured.

"And there might be others," she added. "So keep your eyes peeled for oddballs."

"Will do," I said eagerly, thinking that this might be a lot of fun because the train was full of *oddballs*.

"Do you really think Spizz might follow you?" I asked, because it was an eerie thought.

"Could be," she said with a shrug. "Earlier I passed a door and I thought I heard him talking to himself. I knocked on it but it was just a motion-sick old lady moaning, and I ended up having to take her temperature."

"Is she still alive?" I asked. "You know those old ladies don't last long once you pay them a visit."

"You'll pay for that remark," she threatened, then lifted her head and hammered her whiskery chin into my ear again.

I whimpered. It felt like I'd been kicked by a horse.

"Respect your elders," she advised. "My heart is still broken from those old ladies being murdered—but I'll feel better after I cast my harpoon into that white whale!"

"Is that why you brought that pistol in your purse?" I dared to ask. "To shoot Spizz?"

I winced as I waited to get smacked on the head again.

"As a matter of fact, it is," she replied. "I told you I'm going to kill him, and when I get a chance I'll put that bullet right through his heart and that will be the end of the last chapter of his history—plus now I'll make a few bucks off the reward."

"Would you agree to let me hold the gun for you?" I offered, and extended my hand as if I were a doctor and she was a mental patient.

She thought about it for a minute. "Yes," she said. "That's a good idea. Your hands are more steady than mine so I expect you'll be a better shot."

"That's not what I meant," I said. "I want to keep the gun so we *don't* shoot it."

"Your mother said you had to do anything I asked

of you," she reminded me. "Don't let your mother down."

"She didn't mean I had to murder someone for you," I replied.

"Then forget it," she said stiffly. "I'll use the gun myself. There are six bullets in it and I'm bound to plug him with one of them even if I have to pull the trigger with my toe."

"What if you shoot me by mistake? Or some other person?" I asked.

She cocked her head to one side and smiled coyly. "I'll just make sure I'm alone with him," she said. "In fact, it would be perfect if you would pry open one of the outside doors between the sleeper cars and then he and I could take a romantic stroll and I could pretend to kiss him between the cars but instead when he closed his eyes I could shoot him in the gut and he could fall out the door and roll down the track bed and into the bushes and the rodents would eat his carcass and that would be that!"

"Are you joking?" I asked, thinking that Mom was right. Miss Volker was talking crazy talk.

"I don't joke about murder," Miss Volker said, "but for the moment I can see that you are not in the right mood to be cooperative. And in the meantime let's go to the observation car and enjoy the scenery."

I shifted my hands to just under her stiff shoulders and pushed her straight above me so I could look at her face-to-face. "Can't I just stay in my room and read?" I asked.

She glanced over my shoulder at the comic book on my bed. The garish cover showed the civilized Dr. Jekyll in a tuxedo while the evil Mr. Hyde hovered menacingly over his shoulder like a rancid shrunken head. He was so moldy-looking that I could feel my nose itch.

"That's junk!" she declared, and snapped at it with her square old teeth. "I bet that's how you read *Moby-Dick*!"

"Illustrated Classics comics aren't junk," I countered, feeling a little embarrassed. "And *Dr. Jekyll and Mr. Hyde* really makes you think about what kind of person you are. It's about a doctor with a split personality—one is good and one is evil and they both live inside a single man. I think I'm like that too."

She raised her skeletal hand up over her head and turned the thin edge of it toward me as if it were a meat cleaver. "I'll give you a split personality," she threatened. "Only they'll both be bad. Now push me up onto my feet."

I waited a moment until I caught my breath, and when the train tilted back in the other direction I shoved her away from me with all my might. But it wasn't enough. She elevated about a foot above me and hovered wild-eyed and defiantly against gravity before she came crashing back down with her whale-sized forehead slamming flat against my nose.

The pain brought tears to my eyes. "That really hurt," I sniveled.

"Suck it up and be a man for a change," she ordered, exhaling up my nose as if she were trying to resuscitate me. The stinky fumes from her breath nearly knocked me out.

"Have you been drinking?" I asked in return.

"Only one glass of red wine," she replied. "I had to order something while I waited for you."

"Well, maybe you shouldn't drink wine," I suggested, "because now you can't stand up."

Just then the train snapped back the other way and I gave her a push, and at the same time she jerked her head and shoulders back and just barely staggered up and off of me.

"I'm perfectly sober," she replied in a dignified tone while adjusting her black dress, which had climbed up her thighs so I could see where she had rolled her old-lady support stockings down like two tan doughnuts above her knees. "Now show some manners and stop staring at a single woman's chicken legs and meet me in the lounge," she ordered. "Pronto! I have something juicy to say."

"About what?"

"That's for me to know and you to find out," she said mysteriously.

"Be right there," I fired back, and sat up.

As Miss Volker leaned on the doorjamb to steady herself the train swayed wildly back and forth along a stretch of uneven tracks. Then, in an abrupt roller-coaster spasm, we snapped around another tight curve and she swung out of the doorway like an unhinged clock pendulum and I heard her irritated cries and clomping old-lady heels as she caromed off the compartment doors and down the hallway like a scuttling lobster.

I stood and rubbed my sore ear long enough to get some blood back into it, then carefully shuffled across the linoleum floor in my slippery socks. I grabbed onto the towel rack to secure myself and stood in front of my miniature sink, which was the size of an old porcelain soup bowl. I looked up into my book-sized mirror. My ear was bright red and still creased over like a paper flower, but it was my throbbing nose that really worried me.

Oh cheeze, I thought. Not another bloody nose! I carefully twisted my little finger halfway up my right nostril as if it were a blood dipstick. But before I could pull it out and check for a leak I heard Miss Volker's grating, Klaxon voice growl out above the clacking wheels, "Jack-ie! I'm wait-ing!"

I pulled my unbloody finger out of my nose. "Be right there!" I hollered, then ran my hand over my prickly hair. I pulled in my stomach and more or less tucked my white shirt down into the scratchy winter-wool trousers Mom had picked out for me at the Norvelt tag sale.

As I stepped into the corridor I looked to the left, and then to the right. She was gone. I kept my door key on a string around my neck because there were moth holes in the old pants pockets. The string was pretty short, so I dropped to my knees and pulled the key out from around the neck of my shirt and locked the door. I hopped up before someone, maybe the secret detective, saw me and thought I was a criminal trying to jimmy the lock. Then I went skittering down the corridor while yelping, "Ouch! Ouch! Ouch!" There were a lot of nasty splinters on the oak floors.

7

I really did need my shoes back but I still couldn't find the old steward who had taken them. Maybe he had returned them to the wrong person. I do have big feet for my size, so he could have given them to a small adult by mistake.

I pranced on my tiptoes down the sleeper-car hallways. The roughed-up wooden floor was like walking on a bed of toothpicks. I entered the observation car. It was like a glassy white cocoon. The wet snow had stuck to all the wraparound windows on the sides and roof, and the light inside the car was soft and pearly. I couldn't see anything outside. I had a Classics Illustrated version of *Twenty Thousand Leagues Under the Sea* and I felt like I was standing in the submarine cockpit of the

Nautilus, which Captain Nemo had disguised as a gigantic white narwhal that he used to attack and destroy the battleships of warring nations. Like Miss Volker, he hated war too. The rocking movement of the train made me think we were surging through rough water looking for ships to sink.

It was all so magical until I spotted Miss Volker. She was sitting at a small round table that was still cluttered with the remains of the previous diner's supper. I took a seat across from her. She was hunched toward me and I was startled to see her sobbing into what I thought was a wadded-up napkin, but when I looked closely it was really a crumpled slice of white bread she had lifted from the top of a partly gnawed sandwich.

"I should tell you something important," she said between her halting breaths, which rose and fell like waves on the ocean.

"Are you ill?" I asked. She *was* old. Old enough to go insane or drop dead at any moment—or even to shoot someone with that big silver pistol in her purse.

She sniffed in my direction and shook her head. "No," she whispered, and dabbed at her eyes with the sandwich bread.

"Are we on the wrong train or something?" I asked. I couldn't see out the snow-packed windows but could feel us slowing down. "Like, are we headed to Canada instead of Florida?" I pressed my face against an open spot on the window where the snow had slipped off. At any moment I thought I might catch sight of either a polar bear or an alligator, but we were just moving through a woodsy patch.

"No," she said quietly, and pulled herself upright as she had slid downward on the red vinyl seat. "We're headed south."

"Then tell me what is on your mind," I said with concern. "Because one minute you are angry with me, and the next minute I find you crying into a slice of used bread."

"It was that silly comic of yours," she sniffed.

"If it bothers you that much, I can throw it away," I offered. "Really, I'm sorry. I'm not supposed to read them anyway."

"Keep the comic. It's the story that upset me, because I am like Jekyll and Hyde," she admitted. "On one hand I feel like saving all of mankind and spreading peace around the globe like Mrs. Roosevelt, and on the other hand I have Captain Ahab's obsessive desire to murder that big white Spizz of a whale. But I can't share my inner conflict with you because it might put your life in danger—so forget I mentioned anything."

"My life won't be in danger," I said, thinking she was just being her overly dramatic self. "We're just sitting on a train. It's not as if we're lying across the tracks."

"Trains can be dangerous," she said gravely, and with her curled fingers she pressed the clammy bread against the contours of her face as if she were casting a plaster death mask. "Our fourteenth president," she sputtered as she began to clumsily paw the pasty bread from her face, "lost his third son, cute little Benny, on a train that crashed and killed him instantly. The boy's grieving mother was never the same and hid herself on the upper floors of the White House while writing guilt-ridden letters to dead little Benny, begging for his forgiveness. Nobody could tell her that trains weren't *dangerous*."

"Well, I don't want to end up like Benny, so if what you have to say is so dangerous then you don't have to tell me," I said calmly, and then I smiled like a sympathetic guard in a mental institution.

I slowly reached forward with one hand and plucked a row of dangling, drippy bread beads off her quivering chin, then with my other hand I scampered blindly under the table in a luckless effort to locate a dropped napkin.

Suddenly Miss Volker stomped her hard shoe down onto my knuckles as she dabbed at her eyes with the wad of soggy bread.

"Steward!" she suddenly bawled out so sharply that everyone spun their heads in our direction as if she had been stabbed.

I hunched down into my seat and exhaled like a wounded accordion as I rubbed my throbbing hand with my good one. I turned my face toward the window, which was now like a snow-backed mirror, and spied on the reflected faces of the people behind me. As I slowly looked from face to face I realized that I was the only kid in the car and that all the other passengers were older, probably retired people who were escaping the miserable northern winter for the southern sun. They were leaning forward and staring at us with that puzzled, slightly squinty look on their owlish faces because they couldn't see or hear very well.

At that moment the ferret-faced man I was trying to avoid rushed into the car and dashed toward our section. "Excuse me," he mumbled after a glancing blow from his hip knocked a woman's glasses off one ear. "Pardon me," he said hastily a moment before he flopped down across from us and wedged himself roughly between the hips of two fusty old men on a bench seat.

In an instant he had a little notebook pressed open against his knee and a mechanical pencil poised above it. He took a deep breath but didn't write anything.

Maybe he really was eavesdropping on us and was now wide-eyed and ready to overhear and record our conversation. If Miss Volker was right, he was a lousy detective.

Miss Volker sneaked a look at him across the aisle. From my position I could see a sly, mischievous smile cut across her lips. It looked as if nice Dr. Jekyll had faded away and wicked Mr. Hyde had bubbled up and was getting the best of her.

"Steward!" Miss Volker called out again in her demanding voice.

The steward was busy delivering a steaming pot of tea and a tiered silver tray of lady fingers and macaroons to another table. He walked smartly over to our table once he'd poured a round of tea for his other guests.

"Yes, ma'am?" the steward asked politely as he flipped his serving tray under his arm and dried his hands on a bar towel that hung neatly tucked into the waist of his starched white trousers. He was a handsome black man with a pencil-line mustache and a heavy accent, and he was the first Southerner I had ever heard address a woman as "ma'am."

When I read that word in the Classics Illustrated *Tom Sawyer*, I pronounced it to myself like a sheep bleating, "Maaaaam!" Now it sounded so charming and polite I had to remember to use it to address my mother if she ever found my BB gun. Saying something to her like "I'm sorry I've been a naughty boy, *ma'am*" sounded like I would get in a lot less trouble than saying "I've been a rotten kid, *Mother*."

"Steward," Miss Volker ordered in her trumpeting voice though he was only two feet away, "may I please have another glass of your excellent red wine!"

"Yes, ma'am," he replied, and reached forward with his tray to first clear the dishes from our table.

"Forget the dishes," Miss Volker sharply insisted, and banged her wrist on the edge of the table. "Just get the wine!"

He stepped back a pace and raised an eyebrow at her as he took a deep breath.

"And don't forget the bendy straw," she reminded him. "I can't trust my hands well enough to hold a glass, and I don't want this young man next to me to drink it because he can't hold his liquor and he tries to kiss me when he's drunk."

I snapped my head around and glared at her. "I am *not* a kissing drunk!" I blurted out.

"So you say," Miss Volker retorted, and batted her eyelashes at me as if she were a cartoon of a crazy old lady.

If people weren't staring at us before, they were now gawking at us as they watched a flirting old lady with clumpy bits of sandwich bread stuck to her face throw a tantrum while waving her arthritic claw-shaped hands in the air like lobster hand puppets. And next to her, with his mouth dropped open, sat a flustered red-faced boy who looked like he wanted to throw himself onto the tracks and join little Benny in the hereafter. And across the aisle from that boy was a possible detective furiously writing in his notebook.

The steward glanced contemptuously at Miss Volker, then his gaze shifted and he stared beyond her and into my wide eyes. He lowered his chin and shrugged as if to ask, "Well?" and I knew he was waiting for me to approve or disapprove her drink order because he had seen plenty of irritable old people who had gone around the bend and were screeching like mad crows for more wine.

Just behind the waiter, the detective nervously flipped through the pages of his notebook. Occasionally he paused to read or correct something he'd written, and then he sped on until he came to a clean page where he jotted down a few more words.

I stared at his pointy face. It was twitchy, and he had wiry, bottlebrush hairs bristling out of his ears and even more hairs poking sharply down from his nose, and covering the dark cleft of his chin was a thatch of crisscrossed hairs as if they were hiding the secret entry to an insect lair.

I leaned across the table and under my breath I asked, "Miss Volker, are you sure you need another glass?"

She rolled her shoulders forward and stuck out her lower lip and made a pouty face. Mom warned me that old people can become difficult. But she didn't warn me that when they get really old they revert back to behaving like bratty children.

"Yes," she replied loudly. "In order to kiss you again I'll *definitely* need another glass of wine."

The ball of soggy white bread slipped out of her cramped hand as if it were a scoop of ice cream that had tipped out of a lowered cone. It rolled slowly across the table and hit the floor with an unpleasant splat.

As I bent over and reached for the wet glob of bread I peeked up at the steward whose composed face had tightened into a politely tense mask. He had other old, fidgety passengers calling for him like a pack of mewing cats wanting to be fed.

"She's the boss," I said as plainly as possible. "And please, whatever you do, don't forget the bendy straw." I smiled in an effort to let him know I was on his side.

He exactly matched the width of my smile with his own, but I could see in his eyes that he didn't require my sympathy. I figured the only side he wished we were on was the *outside* of the train.

He turned on one foot and dutifully sped off toward the rear end of the car, where the clinking wine bottles were secured behind a special stainless steel rack so they wouldn't tip over. I sat up and carefully placed the watery bread ball onto the open face of the abandoned ham sandwich it had come from.

In a moment I heard the sudden pop of a cork pulled from the mouth of a wine bottle.

The strange man across the aisle flinched as if Miss Volker had fired a poorly aimed shot over his head. If he was a detective, his nerves didn't seem steady enough for the unforeseen dangers that came with his job.

It had been a pretty rough time for Miss Volker, so maybe she needed the second glass of wine. Maybe a third. But how could I know for sure? I was a kid, so I didn't know exactly what wine did to old ladies. I always thought it made them extra happy and want to hug babies and pinch their cheeks and talk in cutesy baby talk, but I was wrong. Miss Volker was not the happy-granny type.

"I'll tell you why I need a second glass," she hissed, pressing her hand into her chest and throwing her head back in a tortured pose of grief. "Because I need a second chance at life. Because I haven't been a good person."

Out of the corner of my eye I could see the creepy detective alertly extend his elastic ear in our direction.

"Maybe we should change the subject," I advised

calmly. Then I raised my voice for the detective as I added, "We have a lot of funeral plans to make for your sister."

She sniffed and wiped tears from her cheeks just as the waiter delivered her wine and straw. "Thank you," she graciously replied, pulling herself together. Then, before he could leave, she asked, "May I please have another slice of that extra fluffy sandwich bread? It's so soft on my tired old eyes."

The waiter stared at the puddle of wet bread on the leftover sandwich plate, and his upper lip was curled back with disgust so that I could no longer see his mustache. "Yes, ma'am," he replied as smoothly as before. "I'll be right back with the remainder of the loaf."

This time he didn't attempt to clear the dishes.

"Sweet man," Miss Volker said once he had dashed to the other end of the car.

"He's sweet if you close your eyes and just listen to him," I suggested. "But if you look at his face, he doesn't always look too happy with you."

"Having a split personality seems to be a problem on this train," she replied. "Be careful. A lot of people are two-faced and you never know what a two-faced person is truly thinking."

That was obvious. I glanced over at the detective, who had his head stretched in our direction as if he were a dog smelling a steak. When he caught my eye he gave me a piercing stare.

I quickly turned my gaze back to Miss Volker and tried to pull myself together because my heart was pounding.

"How can you tell who is two-faced?" I asked, without expecting what she next said.

"Because I'm one of them," she replied with her voice loudly ringing out as heartfelt and clear as if she had one hand on a Bible and was ready to tell "the truth, the whole truth, and nothing but the truth." She didn't have a Bible but she hooked her trembling hand over my wrist and held it as firmly as she could. "It takes a two-faced person to know one," she continued to testify. "And I'll tell you another—"

I cut her off. "Miss Volker," I pleaded nervously, "please keep your voice down. And don't say what I think you're going to say. It's not true."

"No!" she said, getting all worked up and shifting about in her seat. "All of those old ladies in Norvelt died by my own hands," she passionately announced, loud enough for everyone in the car to hear. She lifted both of her claw-like hands as evidence and frowned irritably at their useless form. "Every one of those ladies has left this earth because of me."

"Miss Volker, please calm down," I begged. "These

people don't even know what you are talking about—and neither do I."

I had read the Illustrated Classics comic version of *Don Quixote*. Like him, Miss Volker was always on a quest to right the wrongs of the world—especially in Norvelt. But now she was suddenly confessing to committing all the wrong done in Norvelt, and I felt like her faithful companion, Sancho Panza, trying to clean up her mess.

"She drank too much wine," I blurted out to those who were staring at us. "Way too much!"

"Rubbish," she said bravely, and puffed out her chest. "This is not the wine talking. I want the whole world to know what evil I've done!"

Just then the train abruptly bucked back and forth with such force the packed snow slid clean off the observation windows to suddenly reveal the bright outside world. Everyone gasped. It was as if stage curtains had been pulled aside to expose Miss Volker's startling confession.

I didn't know about the whole world, but when I checked on the man with the notebook, he was writing so quickly I thought his pencil point would set the paper on fire.

Luckily the steward arrived with a plate stacked high with sliced white bread.

"As you requested, ma'am," he said with a polite nod of his head. For an instant he cut his eyes toward me as if to say, "Good luck with your mad granny."

The moment he sped off to his lunch station, Miss Volker sat back and squinted intently at my face as if she were trying to read the small letters on an eye chart. "You better wipe your proboscis on a piece of this bread," she suggested. "Your nose problem has returned."

After what she just announced, I thought as I reached for a slice, it's a wonder my nose didn't explode like a bloody hand grenade.

I held the bread under my nostrils as if it were a folded handkerchief. When I removed it, there was a glowing red circle of blood in the middle of the white bread. It looked just like the Japanese flag my dad brought home from the war.

The moment Miss Volker saw the blood she hopped up and pointed her claw at me and now directly addressed her audience, whose puzzled members were still murmuring about her last outburst. "Look at the blood of shame running down this boy's face. He is my accomplice in murder!"

The detective gasped and opened his mouth so wide I could count the fillings in his uneven back teeth. At the same time he pressed down so hard on his pencil the point snapped and shot past us and ticked off the little table lampshade. Then he looked directly toward me with such concentration I knew he was trying to forge his way through the labyrinth of my evil mind and enter the blackness of my old-lady-murdering heart. My brain began to throb as he slowly nodded his head up and down as if what Miss Volker said about me added up to exactly what he too had concluded—that I was her secret accomplice at murder, not Spizz. And who wouldn't believe her? Not just because I was dressed up as Spizz when Mrs. Custard ate that cookie and bit the dust, but also because at that moment every person in the train car was staring at the blood spurting out of my nose and down over my lips and chin and dripping onto the dishes.

I opened my mouth to speak but Miss Volker cut me off.

"The blood is the mark of his guilt!" she hollered out, pointing one bent hand toward me.

A woman called out to the steward, "Is this a joke, or some kind of theatrical game?"

But the steward didn't answer. He trotted toward me with his bar napkin in hand.

"Don't worry, son," he said, fussing over me with the napkin and wiping blood from my face. "You'll be just fine." But as he dipped the napkin in a glass of water and continued to mop my face, his nervous eyes said the opposite. "You'll be just fine," he repeated.

I didn't believe him.

"Is there a doctor on this train?" I asked.

"For you or for you-know-who?" he whispered, tilting his head in Miss Volker's direction.

"Me," I said. "She's beyond helping."

"Steward," Miss Volker demanded, and stamped her foot down for extra attention. "Please take my wineglass and the rest of the bottle to my room."

The moment he withdrew to get the bottle of wine she winked at me and under her breath whispered, "Oh, by the way, was that *juicy* enough for you?"

"Why are you pretending that we killed the old ladies when you think it was Spizz?" I whispered back.

"Because they'll just arrest him somewhere and that's not good enough. I want to catch him first and make him suffer, and then I want to kill him myself."

"Well, did you ever think Spizz wants to kill us first?" I suggested. "Maybe he's tracking *us* down."

"Then he'll step right into my trap," she said, nodding smugly as she patted the side of her purse.

"Remember, Mr. Greene said there might be other suspects," I said, trying to reason with her.

"Captain Ahab knew there were a lot of fish in the sea," she countered, "but there was only one white whale."

Then she stood and marched unevenly down the car and toward her roomette.

I quickly turned and looked toward the detective.

He pointed toward his nose but he really meant I should take care of my own nose, which was still dripping. I pointed right back at his nose but my message was different.

"Don't be so nosy," I mouthed.

8

I needed tissues. The men's toilets were down the hall from the dining car, and since I didn't have shoes on I had to enter a narrow stall wearing just my socks, which was pretty bad but not as bad as if I took them off and walked in barefoot. I plopped down on the lowered seat cover and lifted my feet off the floor. I unrolled two piles of toilet paper and with my feet still raised I wrapped the toilet paper around them as if I were preparing an Egyptian mummy for burial. I had just lowered my feet onto the floor when a man entered the next stall. I quietly breathed two or three times but he knew I was in there.

After he dropped his pants and heavily settled himself onto his seat he knocked on the wall between us as if it were the front door of my house.

"Hey, neighbor," he said in a muffled voice from the other stall, "let me introduce myself." He sounded vaguely familiar even though it was obvious he was holding something over his mouth. "I'm the second detective you might have been expecting. I'm the clever one. The one who hears everything you say, but you never see him until it's too late—like right now."

I pulled more toilet paper off the roll and tightly squeezed my nose, which was still leaking. "My mother warned me not to talk to strange men in bathroom stalls," I said, sounding like a kazoo. "She said it's *unhygienic* and dangerous."

"Don't you think it would be far more dangerous if I climbed over this partition to speak to you in *your* stall?" he asked in a logical voice. I couldn't see his face but I could imagine his sick smile as he chuckled after his own joke.

"Okay," I quickly replied. "We can talk. But stay on your side."

"That's a deal," he agreed, and I heard him strike a match and start puffing on a cigarette. "You want a smoke?" he asked.

"I don't smoke, or drink," I stated.

"Well, that's two out of three," he replied.

"What's the third?" I asked.

"Murder," he said bluntly. "The day after Mrs.

131

Custard died we found an open tin of 1080 in Mr. Spizz's office. What do you know about that?"

"I already went over this with the police," I said.

"Let me tell you the difference between me and the police," he explained in a hard voice. "The police arrest people only after they slowly find out the truth. But I like to work a little faster, so I just hurt people when they don't tell the truth right away, and that speeds up the process and then I get the reward money and everyone is happy—except for the killer. So tell me what you saw."

"Well," I said, starting to talk right away because I believed he meant what he said about hurting people. "I had heard someone in Spizz's old office that night. Someone was in there just before Mrs. Custard died and again later, right after she died."

"Are you sure you aren't overlooking the possibility that it was you in that office?" he suggested. "You could have popped the tin of 1080 open, made the poison cookie, and given it to Mrs. Custard—after all, you said in the police report that you gave her a cookie."

"I told the police I gave her an *Oreo*," I stressed. "Not a poison Thin Mint! I think it was Spizz who was in his old office, but I was too afraid to open the door and check for myself so I can't say for sure."

"That is your alibi?" he said doubtfully. "That you

were *too afraid* to poke your nose into the office and catch Spizz in the act of preparing a deadly treat? So you didn't see him, but yet you're suggesting it was him? Ha! Kid, that is your alibi? Believe me, they've sent murderers to the electric chair for less than killing old ladies, so why don't you tell the truth? It was you."

"You don't scare me," I said boldly.

"But you should be scared," he replied, "plenty scared. You ever hear of George Stinney?"

"Who's that?" I asked.

"A nice innocent kid who was only fourteen when he got the electric chair for the murder of two girls that maybe he did or didn't commit."

"I don't know anything about that," I said, and dabbed at my nose.

"He was so small," the detective continued in a sorrowful voice as he drew on his cigarette. "He was about your size. They had to use a Bible for a booster seat on the electric chair."

"I don't want to talk to you anymore," I said.

"Yes you do," he insisted. "Because you don't want to be arrested for something you didn't do, which is why you should tell me how Miss Volker did it."

"She didn't kill anyone," I replied. "She always takes care of people."

"Depends on how you define *takes care of*," he said.

"I know it must be hard on you to realize that Miss Volker is a murderer. It's certainly easier to believe that Spizz did it all on his own, but think about it—did he? Could he, without her knowing? She put the cookies together. She signed off on their death certificates and had the ladies cremated before they could have an autopsy for poison. She had 1080 all over her house. And the last lady, Mrs. Custard, she was murdered like all the rest. Sure, Spizz was in town, but he needed a helper—he needed someone to go into the office and get the 1080 and deliver it to him. He was certainly too afraid of being seen at the Community Center. So who do you think went into his old office and got the poison? It had to be *her*—his girlfriend. They are a deadly duo."

"But her *hands*," I said. "She couldn't use them."

"You mean she couldn't use them for *long*." He pressed forward, breathing hard behind whatever masked his mouth. "Think to when she grabbed you by the back of the neck—were her hands warm?"

He didn't wait for me to answer. I was too shocked that he had seen that to say anything.

"Yes they were," he said, "because I went into her house and she had cooked her hands in wax. The pot on the stove was still hot and I'm guessing that her hand was still a little warm and flexible when she grabbed your neck, otherwise she couldn't grab you because her hand would have been a cold claw."

"I can't remember," I said, feeling trapped.

"Of course not," he rapidly answered. "You were taken by surprise. You were scared. Think about it."

He smoked his cigarette while I sorted through so much he had said, and some was true. But Miss Volker cooked her hands a lot because the heat wore off in about ten minutes. If she was in Spizz's old office she might have been trying to find the 1080 and dispose of it. When Mrs. Custard unexpectedly returned, it ruined Spizz's love plan. Surely he wanted Mrs. Custard dead so Miss Volker would again become the last old Norvelt lady alive and have to marry him. That was the deal they had made. Plus, according to Mrs. Custard, a man who looked like my Spizzy grandfather gave her the cookie to eat right before Bunny and I arrived. That made sense, because Mrs. Custard said I looked like a junior Spizz. Now this detective was trying to say that Miss Volker helped Spizz—but with all her ranting about running a harpoon through Spizz I did not believe she would ever help him.

"You are all wrong," I finally replied. "It has to be Spizz acting on his own."

"Well, I respect you for trying to protect your lady friend. Nobody likes a snitch. So if you won't tell me how she did it, let's try a new approach to this conversation. I have a deal to make with you," he said, once again trying to sound as nice and friendly as he could behind his muffled voice. "It's a good deal. It will keep you out of trouble and make you some real money—cash money."

"I don't need a deal," I replied. "I'm telling the truth, so I'm not in trouble."

"Well, just listen to my offer," he continued. "There's this book, *Strangers on a Train*, where two troubled guys meet by chance on a train—just like you and me are doing. Anyway, in the book the two guys start to talk about their unhappy situations. One guy has a wife he doesn't like and the other guy has a father who won't share his fortune with him. So after a few glasses of wine one of the guys has a brainstorm and says to the other, 'Hey, I've got a plan.' And he proposes that he kill the other guy's wife and in return the other guy kills the father. 'This way we both get what we want and nobody will guess it is us,' says the first guy. 'We're total strangers. They'll never connect the murders back to us. It's too random. Untraceable.'"

"What's your point?" I asked, trying my best to sound pretty smooth while on my side of the wall my hands were shaking as I was twirling thin coils of toilet paper way up my nose.

"That you and I," he continued, "can be like those two strangers and help each other get what we want and no one will ever have to know."

"I think I want to remain a stranger," I said.

"Relax. Don't worry so much," he replied. "Here's my offer. I'll accept your word of honor that you and Miss Volker are innocent, and in return you just tell me where Spizz is hiding. I'll take care of him, and then I'll split the reward with you—and there is a lot of money because the relatives were in a foul mood when they found out the life insurance didn't pay one red cent for *murder*."

"I don't know where he is," I said. "He could be on the moon."

"Don't be childish," he said dismissively. "You know he's not on the moon. He's like a hound dog always tracking after Miss Volker—"

"Mister, I don't know for sure who killed all those old ladies," I said, and flushed the toilet like I was getting ready to run out of there.

"I think you know very well who killed them," he said with more bite in his firm voice. "So let me remind you that if we make this deal like two strangers on a train we'll both be happy. I'll get Spizz and the reward. Volker can get away with murder, and you can become a man and fill your pockets with big bucks."

"I don't want the money," I said. "I'm a kid. And she didn't kill anyone anyway."

"Remember poor George Stinney," he reminded me.

"Being a kid is no alibi for murder. I'd hate to tell the police that you helped Spizz. That would make you an accessory to the crime. Instead, think about this. The reward money could help you and your family get a new start in Florida."

"How do you know about Florida?" I asked too quickly, and I could feel my heart racing, because now I thought he *did* know too much—he *was* the smart detective.

"You could buy your mother a new blue dress," he said smoothly. "Maybe help your dad get seed money to start a business in Miami and move out of Norvelt for good. Maybe get a real doctor to fix your nose."

"How do you know this stuff?" I asked.

"I'm a detective," he said confidently. "Knowing other people's business is my business."

Just then he slipped a twenty-dollar bill under the stall. "For your comic-book collection," he said. "This is just the tip of the iceberg."

I looked at the twenty. Classics Illustrateds cost fifteen cents each. Twenty dollars was a lot of cash for me, but I didn't touch it. Besides, my nose was beginning to work again and the money smelled—smelled like rot and bathroom chemicals all at the same time.

"Hey," he said, "I'm out of toilet paper. Throw some over the top of the stall."

I thought about it.

"Use the twenty," I said.

"Don't be a smart-ass," he snapped back at me without humor. "Just give me some paper."

"Will you leave me alone then?" I asked.

"For a little while," he agreed.

"Mr. Greene at the newspaper said there are other suspects," I said.

"Maybe so," he replied, "but that idiot Spizz is the only one who should get the electric chair. That kid, George Stinney, never killed those girls. But he got the chair anyway. Sometimes justice isn't fair," he said forlornly. "It would be terrible for the wrong person to get the chair—especially an old lady and a boy."

I didn't even know who George Stinney was, but electrocuting a kid for something he didn't do scared me.

I unrolled a wad of tissues for myself, then pulled the roll off the spindle and lobbed it over the top of the stall.

I heard his quick hand snatch it before it hit the floor. "Thanks, kid," he said. Suddenly his voice sounded different. He must have dropped whatever he held over his mouth in order to catch the toilet paper.

A moment later he flushed and quickly opened his door, and in an instant he pressed his shoulder against my door to pin me in. "Remember, kid," he said with his voice muffled again. "I know what you look like. I'll always spot you before you even sniff me. If you have some information for me, just hang the tail end of a white handkerchief out of your back pocket. I'll see it. I'll always be tailing you. That will be our signal that you are ready to talk. See you around." Then, just as quickly as he had arrived, he vanished, without even washing his hands.

I stayed sitting on the seat with my head tilted back to let the blood coagulate and I was going over what had just happened and what I should do next when somebody took the empty stall. I thought maybe the detective had come back to say something more. Maybe he had another threatening story to tell me about a kid who was framed for a crime he didn't commit.

"I haven't changed my mind," I said firmly.

Surprisingly it was a different man who replied. "*Gantos boy,*" whispered the sandpaper voice of Mr. Spizz. "You are in over your head."

"Spizz!" I said happily. It made me feel so good to hear a familiar voice even if it was the man who might get me the electric chair. Then I made a little joke. "I'm not in over my head," I said, "because I haven't flushed yet."

"Ha!" he laughed. "But what I mean is, Miss Volker is taking you for a ride and you are too blind to see it.

Now she's going around blaming Mrs. Custard's murder on me too."

"That's because you probably did it," I insisted. "You came back to kill Mrs. Custard. I heard you that night in your old office."

"I admit I was in the office," he said earnestly. "But someone had been there before me and opened the 1080 and spilled it on the floor. I was waiting to meet the one person who could clear my name of murder when I heard you come into the Community Center—and you called out, 'Is someone in there?' But then you got scared and left, and when the coast was clear I sneaked out just behind you. That's when I saw who grabbed you by the neck. It was your girlfriend, Miss Volker, and I think she was the one who had gone to my office in the first place to get the 1080."

"But Mrs. Custard said you had gone to her house," I replied, poking a hole in his explanation. "And she said you gave her the Girl Scout cookie."

"Nonsense!" he said angrily. "I didn't go to her house. I returned to town to run off with Miss Volker because I won the bet—she was the last old Norvelt lady left."

"You are lying," I said. "The truth is you killed Mrs. Custard, and Miss Volker can't stand you."

"You have it all wrong, kid. She hasn't told you the whole story. She loves me. After I wrote that phony confession to protect her I ran off and have been hiding in the Glades. I was going to sneak back and marry her because she was the last old Norvelt lady. We didn't expect another old Norvelt lady to return and that messed up our deal. But then Miss Volker knocked off Mrs. Custard so she would remain the last old Norvelt lady and marry me—the man of her dreams. Anything else she tells you about me is a lie."

"You're the one who is lying," I shot back. "Miss Volker wouldn't marry you—she wants to send you to the bottom of the ocean."

"Kid, you have a lot to learn about love. She loves me as much as she hates me," he said bluntly. "You'll see. But remember this as we all head to Florida, I'm on your side."

"I find that hard to believe," I replied.

"To prove it, let me give you a little gift." In a moment he slid my shoes under the stall.

"Where'd you get those?" I asked, and snatched them up and onto my lap before he could pull them back.

"They were in her room," he replied. "Your girlfriend's been holding out on you. She's not telling you the truth."

I didn't believe him. He must have stolen them from the steward who was going to polish them. I reached forward and ripped the toilet paper wrapping off my feet. When I went to put on one of my shoes I saw a folded-up piece of train stationery inside.

"You see the note," he said, knowing I would. "Give it to her. And if you're smart, keep an eye out on that pistol she has. She stole it from Mrs. Custard's kitchen drawer. I saw her do it when I was spying through the kitchen window."

Maybe I did believe him because suddenly I blurted out, "Keep an eye on the guy who was just in here. He's dangerous."

He laughed hard at that last bit. "I have one word for that smelly bum," Spizz said, then he flushed the toilet. The water gushed loudly and when it settled back down Spizz was gone.

I looked at the note. It was written in Esperanto. I couldn't make out any part of it except for one name, *Huffer*. What could that mean? I thought. Maybe it had something to do with the casket. After all, Miss Volker had hired Mr. Huffer to join us in Florida to help prepare her sister's body for a return to Norvelt.

But for now it felt so good to have my shoes back on my feet I busted out of the bathroom stall like a bucking bronco and ran crazily down the train hallways kicking at splinters and pounding down nail heads with my heels. I didn't know who invented shoes but I wanted to kiss them!

When I got to Miss Volker's door I just slipped the

note through the bottom crack and kept clippity-clomping down the hall to the safety inside my own roomette. Quickly I set the dead bolt then dropped to my knees, pulled out my key, and double-locked the door. I untied my shoes and peeled my dirty socks off and dropped them into my sink of soapy water. As I brushed my teeth in front of the mirror I could see the reflection of the cover of *Dr. Jekyll and Mr. Hyde* spread out across my bunk, except in the mirror the letters in the title were reversed, just like the character kept reversing in the story. One minute I went from reading about Jekyll turning into Hyde and the next moment it switched to Hyde turning into Jekyll.

I felt the same way myself. One moment I was certain of who I was, and the next moment I was feeling like someone I had never met before in my life. How did I go from being a regular boy from Norvelt to being a boy threatened with the electric chair for murder, and then back to just being a plain old boy washing his socks in the sink? Dr. Jekyll didn't know the truth about himself and maybe I didn't know the truth about myself either. After all, look what I did to poor Mrs. Custard. I had become her Mr. Hyde when I dressed up like Mr. Spizz. I always thought of myself as a nice boy, but I wasn't as nice as I thought, and no one else was either.

As I rinsed the soap out of my socks I kept peeking into the mirror to see if I had turned into my evil self, but I just saw the boyish face I knew so well. "Be the solid man your mother wants you to be," I said to myself. As I hung my socks on the towel rack I could hear her steady voice in my head, "Don't jump to conclusions. Think it all through and you won't fall to pieces."

But as I stepped into my pajamas I could only hope that a different me didn't step out of them in the morning.

9

Sleeping on a train is like being gently rocked back and forth in a cradle. Waking up is more like being tossed out of one. I was curled up into a ball of infant bliss when the head-banging started against my door. I knew who it had to be.

"Miss Volker," I called out, and threw my covers to one side. "I'm coming."

I dropped to my knees in front of the door and unlocked it with my key. I remembered how she had rammed me the last time, so this time I carefully slid the dead bolt halfway and got into a position to leap to one side. At that moment, she hit the door so hard the dead bolt tore loose and she bore down on me like the carved maiden on the bow of a whaling ship. She rammed her wood-hard head directly into my chest. The air rushed out of my lungs and we both fell back onto my bunk. Not this again, I thought.

"I just read Spizz's note!" she said in a panic. "Did you read it?"

"No. I can't . . . read . . . Esperanto," I wheezed with my last thin wisp of air.

"I'll teach you someday," she said hastily, then turned her head to see if she had been followed. "But for now we have to get off this train."

I agreed, and wanted to blurt out my news about the second detective and Spizz, but without air I just gummed my words like actors in silent films.

"What are you? A ventriloquist's dummy? Say something!" she demanded. Then in an effort to push herself off of me she pressed her claws down on my windpipe.

I raised my hands and used my fingers to give clues, as if I were playing charades and trying to act out the words for "choking to death."

"Are you using sign language for the deaf?" she asked. "Because I think you just spelled out 'white whale.'"

I shook my head.

"Something to do with the *Pequod*?" she guessed.

I nodded.

"I agree. We better get ready to abandon ship," she

said, and removed her hands from my neck and scooted over to the edge of the bed. I felt like a criminal who had just received a last-second gallows pardon.

I staggered onto my feet and raised my arms up above my head and down again, and up again and down again. As the air was pumped back into my flattened lungs I made a loud rasping noise like a braying donkey.

"This is no time to sound like an ass," she said crossly. "If you have something to say, then just *say* it."

"Spizz and the second detective"—I gasped hoarsely—"they are on the train."

"I know," she replied. "Spizz slipped a note under my door when I was asleep."

"That was me!" I cried out. "The second detective and Spizz followed me to the bathroom after you got drunk and announced that I was a murderer and . . ."

"I wasn't *drunk* and you can tell me your news later. For now Spizz is going to make a run for it once we get to Washington."

"Perfect," I replied. "Let him run. We'll get rid of Spizz and the detectives and continue to Florida to meet up with Mr. Huffer and return your sister's body to Norvelt like you planned."

"You keep missing the point," she replied sharply. "We want the detectives to follow *us*. That's why I announced we killed the old ladies. Now that note changes everything. If the detectives arrest Spizz, I'll never have a chance to kill him myself." She slumped back onto the bed.

"Just let the detectives do their job and arrest him," I insisted.

"We have to get to Spizz before they do," she persisted, popping back up. "Now you do your job. Get dressed and start packing. Remember, Mrs. Captain Ahab took an oath to follow her white whale to the end of the earth."

"You don't really plan to kill him," I said daringly. "You're like Bunny Huffer. She says she wants to bury me but she really wants to kiss me."

"Open your eyes!" she shot back. "Spizz is a murderer, and that weird troll-doll girlfriend of yours does want to bury you—as soon as you purchase one of her father's abnormal caskets!"

"Close your eyes," I said in an effort to change the subject. "I have to take off my pajama bottoms."

"Don't worry," she replied, and looked me up and down with her X-ray eyes. "After you fell into the septic tank, your mother gave me a detailed description of what you look like naked from the waist down."

"What!" I shouted, and jumped like I'd stepped on a nest of splinters. "Why'd she do that?"

"She wanted advice about the nasty red skin rash on your rear that she claims is in the shape of Italy."

"Stop!" I insisted, and pointed at her mouth. "Don't talk."

Suddenly I knew there was only one way to end this conversation. I yanked down my pajama bottoms and bent over in her direction. "See, I'm fine," I insisted, and gave her a good look. "Nothing has *spread*. I don't have a map of Italy on my butt."

She cocked her head to one side and hummed as if she were contemplating a medical oddity. "I'd say it's more in the shape of an octopus. But don't be embarrassed," she replied calmly. "A lot of infirm elders get exotic rashes on their backsides from poor hygiene and dirty diapers. Sometimes even I get . . ."

"*Don't* say it," I ordered, and pointed my finger at her mouth. "No! This conversation about *my* bottom is bad enough. I don't want to think about *your* bottom."

"Your loss," she said in a sultry voice, and batted her eyes at me as I pulled up my drawers. "Now, do you have the ointment I gave your mother?" she asked. "I can rub some on your rash before it wraps its grasping tentacles around your sensitive parts."

"I put some on last night," I lied as I snaked my arms through my shirtsleeves, then quickly buttoned up.

"What else did Spizz say in the note?" I asked.

"Something about Huffer and the casket for my sister, but I couldn't make out the rest," she said, sounding vague. "Spizz was always a lousy student of Esperanto."

"Maybe you should slow down and *read the note* again!" I suggested a little too harshly. "Maybe there is something important Spizz is trying to tell us about the casket—you know, like at the end of *Moby-Dick*, when Ishmael uses a casket as a life raft."

"Don't tell me about *Moby-Dick*," she arrogantly snapped back. "You only read the comic-book version. Besides," she added, "Huffer is always hopeful someone will drop dead. Maybe he's bringing an extra casket for Spizz after I do him in."

"You are a big talker," I jabbed back, and pulled up my itchy wool pants and fastened my belt. "If you wanted to harpoon Spizz it seems you had years to do it in Norvelt."

She dismissed the thought. "Too many witnesses there," she replied. "But soon I'll get him alone and I'll bury him where he'll never be found."

"That reminds me," I said, as I put my shoes on. "Spizz found my shoes. He told me you had been hiding them from me."

"That's a whale of a lie," she declared. "And you

must be dumb as a post. He knows that if you don't have shoes and I don't have hands then we can't follow him. We'll be adrift without a sail or a paddle."

She was right. But I didn't say so because I could feel the train slowing a bit. We were hours behind schedule. The train had been stopped for much of the night because of some mechanical problem nobody explained to us. When it finally got going again, I didn't feel a thing. But now it seemed like we had finally reached Washington. I quickly opened my little suitcase and grabbed at my clothes and Classics Illustrateds and pressed them madly into the case and snapped the metal clasps shut.

"I'm going to get your bag and overcoat," I said, rushing my words. "So stay put. I don't want Mrs. Captain Ahab to wander off course."

"Don't forget my half bottle of wine!" she reminded me. "A little grog on the high seas always helps my aim." She winked at me as she patted the outline of the pistol in her cloth pocketbook.

She's lost her compass, I thought as I stepped out into the corridor and walked quickly down the hall.

The view from the train windows flickered by like the frames in an old film. The rising sun cast long beams of light down the wide avenues of Washington, D.C. The rays gleamed along the curbs of snow and spread like a hand with a thousand brilliant fingers. Windows blinked like waking eyes. Roof antennas shone as they stretched their silver branches. Clouds glowed, the sky blued, and shadows turned and fled from the city named after the president who brought this country into the light.

As I watched, the night seemed to vanish into me as easily as Mr. Hyde vanished within Dr. Jekyll. The train moved on but I stood still with a powerful sense of doom. I wanted to call my mother and tell her that Miss Volker had a gun and was out to kill Mr. Spizz, but there was no phone on the train and even if I did talk with her I knew what she would say. At the train station in Greensburg she had put her hands on my shoulders and stooped down to face me. "Remember, you are like her seeing-eye dog. Without you she is helpless. Promise me you will do whatever she says." I had raised my hand like a Boy Scout and repeated, "I promise."

When the train slowed even more, there was a sudden eruption of action as porters hustled luggage through the corridors and rapped on doors while announcing our arrival at "Uoon-yun Staa-tion!"

Some swarthy guy in striped pajamas opened his door and stuck his head out. "Finally!" he groused. "I'm late for last night's dinner with my congressman."

I kept pace with the porters and ducked and dodged

their coming and going until I made it to the next sleeper car.

When I opened Miss Volker's roomette door, I half expected the mysterious second detective to grab me from behind, but it was only my nervous imagination hiding behind the door. I kept thinking about the detective's muffled voice in the toilet stall. When he dropped his handkerchief I was certain I'd heard that voice before. Or was my dad right in telling me that my imagination was a servant to my fears? He could be right. In my daydreams I always seemed to be the victim and not the conqueror.

Miss Volker's suitcase was on her bunk. I threw the corked bottle of wine on top of her lady things, closed and snapped the clasps, then slung her coat over my shoulder and dashed back up the hallway. When I elbowed open my door she had vanished and the train was shuddering to a stop as the brakes were slowly applied.

"Cheeze-us-crust," I muttered. "Where'd Mrs. Captain Ahab sail off to?"

I stuck my head out the doorway and took a quick glance up and down the sleeper car. I didn't see her, so I grabbed my bag as well and followed the porters down the hall until I jumped out the first door that slid open.

I ran down the platform and joined up with the gathering passengers that attempted to enter the wide portals of Union Station.

I pressed myself into the crowd and leaned forward. All around me the shoulders of passengers trying to enter the station jammed up against the shoulders of people equally driven to make their trains. It was as if we were all trapped inside one revolving door. A man shoved me from behind and in turn I shoved the man in front of me until finally, step by step, we stumbled into the station.

Instantly, everyone had a determined expression of knowing where they were going, except for me. My eyes circled wildly once I entered the vast white concourse, but I didn't dare stop.

I followed the people dashing ahead of me. Along the wide corridor, café waiters held out trays of toasted bacon and egg sandwiches and called out for customers. There were baskets of sweet rolls and fritters. Hawkers handed off paper cups of steaming coffee to racing commuters who in turn paid the hawkers as if passing a baton. Newspaper venders announced the headlines.

RUSSIA REMOVES BOMBERS FROM CUBA!
U.S. NAVY BACKS AWAY! WAR UNLIKELY!

All that good news was lost on me because I was trying to spot Miss Volker. I picked up my speed again as my eyes scanned left and right.

Maybe I passed her already, I thought, and spun around. People lurched past me. I didn't spy the creepy little detective or Spizz. If I really was a Seeing Eye dog, I would have spotted them all in a glance.

And then I saw a line of red-capped porters pushing carts of luggage and dollies stacked with wooden crates and other freight. On the very top of one crate was balanced a casket. It gleamed like one of Huffer's special bombproof models—the kind with the glass window on the top that Bunny liked because when the lid was closed you could look in and see if the person was dead or alive. I hoped this one was empty.

On the far side of the casket, I could just see a dark hat bobbing up and down and a thick hand gripping the top edge of the crate underneath to keep it steady.

Suddenly I was knocked off my feet by a commuter rushing for the train platforms. I jumped up and darted sideways between people, slipping like a fish behind and in front of them.

I was closing in on the casket and that's when a pistol fired off somewhere ahead of me. People screamed and ducked down. Someone pointed toward an upper balcony. Others turned abruptly and pointed in the opposite direction. Everyone froze for a moment and began to swivel their necks around to find where the shot had come from as the *crack!* of it echoed sharply back and forth along the massive barrel vault of the station.

I could guess exactly where the bullet came from and it was easy for me to imagine the target! At any moment I expected the crowd to gasp and part and there would be Spizz, dying belly-up like a beached white whale while Mrs. Captain Ahab stood over him with the smoking pistol in one hand and her peg leg jammed into his quivering navel.

And then I heard someone shout, "Oh my God, she's shot!"

A little crowd of people gathered in a horseshoe around a fallen woman and I ran toward them.

I saw the scuffed bottoms of her shoes first. She was stretched out like a swimming-pool diver, with her arms and face flat down on the Union Station floor. When I reached her I dropped to my knees and tucked in next to her shoulder.

"Miss Volker," I cried in a panic as I leaned over her face. "Can you hear me?"

Then I gasped because blood was running out of her

hair and across her forehead. "You've been hit!" I exclaimed in horror.

She rolled her face over and glared up at me as if I was some sort of useless idiot. "Get me up off this filthy floor before the police arrive," she hissed.

"But you shouldn't move," I begged, as she gritted her teeth and struggled up onto one knee. I stood and braced my arm across her thin back to steady her. Blood dribbled out of her ear and seeped into the white lace collar of her sweater.

She clutched my shoulder and raised herself onto her other knee. "Get me on my feet," she panted hastily. "We have to skedaddle out of here."

I turned to a gawking luggage porter and nodded toward our suitcases and her overcoat. "Grab those and lead us to a taxi—we need to get to a hospital now!"

"That's a lot of blood," a man said dramatically, as I lowered my arm around Miss Volker's waist and hoisted her onto her feet.

Once she was upright, we marched behind the porter, who cut a path through the crowd while Miss Volker and I left a trail of bloody footprints behind us.

When we reached the taxi, the porter set our suitcases in the trunk and snappily opened the back door.

I spun Miss Volker onto the vinyl seat and jostled her legs into the cab before slamming the door. I turned and for an instant looked back to where I had last seen the casket, but it was gone.

Quickly I ran around to the far side and opened my door.

"Tip the porter!" Miss Volker hollered out before I could dive inside. "Never stiff a working man."

"Cheeze!" I cried out. I dug into my pocket and yanked out a bill. It was a ten. In the distance I spotted a blue-uniformed cop talking intently to a knot of people just outside the station. A lady turned and jabbed at the air in our direction. The cop nodded.

I shoved the ten at the porter and saw drops of blood on his white-gloved hand. "When that cop arrives," I said breathlessly, "tell him to meet us at the nearest emergency room."

"Yes, sir," he replied. I threw myself into the taxi and slammed the door just as Miss Volker hollered to the driver, "The Lincoln Memorial! And step on it."

"You mean drive to the *hospital*," I cut in. "You've been shot in the face."

"No, *you've* been shot in the face," she replied, correcting me. "Right in the nose, to be exact."

I pulled a handkerchief out of my coat pocket and mopped the blood off my nose and mouth and chin.

Then I looked down at my coat: it was bloody, as were my shirt and hands. My face must have been twisted up into an expression of absolute terror. I began to wildly pat myself all over in an effort to search for my bullet wound.

"Calm down, Chicken Little. You aren't shot. But," she asked, raising a schoolmarm's eyebrow, "which president *was* shot in the Baltimore and Potomac train station in Washington?"

The question seemed crazy to me at that moment but I knew the answer from one of her This Day In History columns in Mr. Greene's newspaper.

"Garfield," I answered with confidence. "President Garfield. He was shot in 1881 on my birthday, July second."

She smiled. "A-plus," she said approvingly, and patted me on the shoulder with her firm hand. "Your mother would be proud. Remember, no matter how bad things become, history always gives you the gift of perspective— basically, make sure the gun is in your hand."

And that's when I smelled the gunpowder coming from her cloth purse. I opened my mouth and Mr. Hyde spoke. He was not in a good mood.

"You told me you'd only fire the gun if you were *alone* with Spizz!" I said, hardly trying to keep my voice down.

She frowned. "When I'm truly aiming for him I will be alone," she replied. "But in this case I wasn't aiming for him."

"Then who?" I asked, still steaming.

"I was creating a distraction. They almost nabbed Spizz," she explained. "I saw that little ferret-faced detective sneaking up on him in the station with the butt end of a gun in his coat pocket. I reached into my purse. I clutched the pistol grip and raised the purse straight up into the air but I was having trouble curling my finger around the trigger. I swear my hands are getting worse. My finger had frozen up, and just then someone bumped into me and I tripped and when I hit the deck the gun went off. The bullet must have shot across the floor."

"What you did was totally criminal," I shouted, scolding her as if I were my mother. "You could have killed someone."

She dismissed my concern with a wave of her hand. "Calm down. By accident, I probably shot the heel off some lady's shoe," she said without concern. "But by design, I sidetracked the detective, and during the confusion I figure Spizz got away."

"If he did escape, how will you ever find him?" I asked.

"The best way to catch a killer is to think like one,"

she replied. "In Spizz's case I don't have to think too hard. I know where he'll end up."

"So he's going to the Lincoln Memorial?"

"No," she scoffed. "History is lost on him. Like a little baby whale, he'll return to his mama's home. But he's so slow we have time to visit the Lincoln Memorial. Since we are in Washington, I can show you something that's not in any of your comic books. It's something about Eleanor, and we can add it to her obituary."

"Aren't we running from the police?" I reminded her, turning around to look out the back window for squad cars.

"Use your head," she advised. "Only the guilty run. If you stand still, the police zip right by you like the Keystone Cops."

It wasn't long before the cab driver pulled into the parking lot at the Lincoln Memorial. As he shifted around in his seat to collect the fare he gave me a bug-eyed look of surprise when he saw the blood.

"Don't worry about the boy," Miss Volker said. "He's tougher than he looks."

I stepped out of the cab and went around to the trunk. The cab driver followed. "Looks like that old lady knocked you out in the first round," he remarked, snickering as he opened the trunk.

"Don't turn your back on her," I advised, and felt some humor water down my anger. "She sucker punched me." I grabbed our bags and her coat. He closed the trunk and Miss Volker and I hiked up to the front of the monument, which was like climbing to the top of a Greek temple.

Once we reached the portico we stared way off to the left but couldn't see the White House because of the trees. I couldn't see the Jefferson Memorial either, but I knew it was not far across the Tidal Basin. Right ahead of me there was no missing the reflecting pool and Washington Monument that stood up ramrod straight like the spine of the nation.

"From this very spot," Miss Volker said, raising her arms to form a circle, "American history forms an unbreakable chain, with each link telling one nation-building story after another."

I turned and looked up at Lincoln.

She followed my gaze. "What do you see when you look up at that man?" she asked with reverence.

"I'm not sure," I said shakily, knowing that she expected me to say something more momentous than "a man sitting in a chair."

"Well, I'll tell you what Lincoln sees when he looks down at you," she replied since she had no patience for ignorance. "He sees a twelve-year-old boy with his mouth hanging open who only knows that Lincoln was born in a log cabin, read books by firelight, became a lawyer, then president, defeated the Confederates, freed the slaves, and was assassinated by John Wilkes Booth at Ford's Theatre."

I lowered my head because she was right. I had only read the fifteen-cent Classics Illustrated version of Lincoln's life.

But suddenly I remembered something else that was hugely historic. "You know the movie *The Day the Earth Stood Still*?" I asked excitedly.

She frowned.

"Well, Klaatu, the visitor from outer space, lands around here, and he comes up to the Lincoln Memorial and reads the Gettysburg Address on the wall and says, 'Those are great words, he must have been a great man.'"

"You are a hopeless pupil," Miss Volker said, gawking at me as if *I* had dropped down from outer space.

"Well, what do you see?" I asked testily.

"A lot. One reason we came here is because we can really talk about how Jekyll and Hyde are like the North and the South. 'A house divided cannot stand,' Lincoln said. And he meant more than just the Union and the Confederacy," she added. "He meant blacks and whites too. The nation had become a Jekyll and Hyde with the South rising up as an evil twin inside the nation to kill off America's highest belief that all men are created equal."

She stamped her foot down on the granite floor.

"The earth has its own axis but the heart and humanity of America pivots at the feet of Lincoln. We are not so much defined by the wars we fight across the globe, but by the wars we have fought within ourselves as a nation. It is here where the people forced democracy to turn the gears of justice. I love Lincoln. He was one of the greatest presidents of this conflicted nation. Look up at him. Look at the statue with his haggard face, slumped shoulders, and tired legs. He's exhausted from carrying on a war in which six hundred thousand Americans died and hundreds of thousands were wounded and maimed. He looks like he already knows John Wilkes Booth is going to end his life."

He did look tired. He was the president, but his stony hands looked like the hard hands of a grave digger.

"You could also say," she continued, "that he looks like a man exhausted by an inner conflict because he is tired from wrestling with his own Jekyll and Hyde. Lincoln did not start out in favor of freeing the slaves. In fact, he spoke against mixing blacks and whites in society, and instead he supported a movement to ship all the slaves back home to Africa. But deeper still, he wrestled with his moral belief that no man should be enslaved by another. And when the abolitionists gathered together and agitated and protested in one voice against slavery, Lincoln changed his mind. His greatness was in listening to the will of the people, and as president he gave all people what they asked for—freedom and equality. Now that is true democracy!"

"It is," I remarked. "If you don't question yourself, you can never change your mind."

"Listen to me," she said, "so I can also *improve* your mind. Sadly, what you don't see on Lincoln's face are the four million slaves that gained their freedom and ended up working for slave wages paid out by the same rich men who had owned them in the first place. Not enough had changed in America after all the war's carnage and suffering. And to their unforeseen surprise, the South came to realize they had actually won the war because they were never defeated in their ugly belief that white people were superior to blacks. Sadly the Civil War went from something that was honorable and full of humanity to something shameful."

She looked up at Lincoln and took a deep breath.

"I hate war as much as he did," she said. "So many do."

"Even my dad doesn't like war," I added. "And he fought in one."

"You'll learn from history," she said firmly, underlining her words with wisdom, "that it's mostly the people who haven't been to war that start them."

Then she cocked her head at me, and her face seemed to freeze up like a cat seeing itself in a mirror. Maybe she was thinking of Lincoln and Garfield and McKinley and wondering what president might be shot next. Maybe she was regretting her vow to shoot Spizz. Maybe Jekyll and Hyde were arm wrestling inside her for the pistol at that moment and they were locked up in a tie.

I took a chance. "Please give the gun to me," I encouraged, "and we can throw it into the Potomac River. It will be better that way."

She gave her head a shake and it seemed the conflict inside her was over. "I'm not quite ready to give you the pistol," she slowly replied, backing away from her better half. "Not yet. I'm getting there—maybe later, but not now. Eleanor had a permit to keep a little protection in her purse when she traveled, and I think I will too."

"Well, you give it some serious thought," I said,

trying not to sound as disappointed as I felt. "Just remember that my mother said we make our best choices about how we live and not about how we die."

"I'll keep that in mind," she remarked, and reached into her purse. "Now turn your back to me," she ordered, "and take a long look at the reflecting pond and beyond."

I did, and as I stood there I thought of that pistol in her purse. I knew she wouldn't shoot me. Not intentionally, but she might fall down again with her hand on the pistol trigger and I'd be bleeding from somewhere other than my nose.

"Now what do you see?" she asked.

I figured it would be best to die while telling the truth. "I cannot tell a lie," I declared, "I see the Washington Monument, and I figure it looks to be the right size harpoon for Mrs. Captain Ahab to defeat the white whale."

She laughed and I turned around to see that her hands were empty. "That's more like the harpoon Washington used on the British," she said, and with a flourish pretended to heave the huge Washington Monument right through the puffed-up belly of mad King George. I bet she could do it too.

"Are we finished with my lesson?" I asked nervously. "We haven't talked about Mrs. Roosevelt's obit yet and I'm a little worried that the real cops will catch up to us."

"Hold your horses," she said, slowly glancing up and down the roads and pathways. "I might be writing an obituary, but these are the moments in history that live forever. This is the site of one of Eleanor Roosevelt's greatest victories over racism and prejudice, so we have to add it."

I had kept the pen she had earlier given to me in the cemetery and now removed it from my jacket pocket. I opened my small suitcase and pulled out the pad of paper I was writing on. I tested the tip and now that the ink was warmer it flowed just fine. "I'm ready," I said.

"On this very spot another battle for freedom was fought within ourselves as a nation. Right here Marian Anderson sang, 'My country 'tis of thee, sweet land of liberty, of thee *we* sing.'

"She changed the 'of thee *I* sing' to '*we*' to include *all* Americans. And do you know why she was up here singing it?"

"No," I said, feeling like a student who skipped his homework.

"Because she was a black woman and was going to sing at Constitution Hall, owned by the Daughters of the American Revolution, but in 1939 they would not let her sing to an integrated audience. They *banned* her because she wanted to sing to all races under one roof. And this is why the great Eleanor Roosevelt resigned her own membership in the D.A.R. 'That's that!' she probably said. 'I've had enough of this evil racism.' I expect she ripped up her membership card and did a little angry dance on the pieces."

With that, Miss Volker did a little dance of her own to illustrate Eleanor's angry jig. But she wasn't finished there. Once she caught her breath she continued to orate. "And as a result Eleanor Roosevelt secretly arranged for Marian Anderson to sing for free at the Lincoln Memorial to a *gigantic* audience of all colors and creeds. Well, she sure showed the D.A.R. ladies something about patriotism!"

"Yep," I said, and pointed across the Tidal Basin toward the Jefferson Memorial. "She reminded them what the Constitution was all about—that all people are created equal."

"A-plus for that," she said, patting me on the shoulder before starting up again. "And to further show just what a great person Marian was—she was a *forgiving* person—in 1943 Marian Anderson was invited back to Constitution Hall to sing because those white D.A.R. ladies realized they had made a huge blunder and angered Eleanor and embarrassed themselves.

"Now, everyone would have understood completely if Marian Anderson had put her foot down and said, 'Forget it, you white old ladies! You insulted me and my race and I'll never forgive you for it.' But she didn't say that. She graciously forgave them and went back to Constitution Hall and sang to an integrated audience and was a huge success.

"Just as Lincoln had his mind turned against slavery by the will of the people, so too did the women of the D.A.R. change their minds when they looked out at the real America—the America made up of races from all around the world—and saw the power of seventy-five thousand people listening to Marian sing at the Lincoln Memorial and millions more listening on the radio, and they were convinced they were wrong. The people had once again gathered to cast a vote and right a wrong—which is how democracy is supposed to work. People have the power. And just last year Marian sang for President Kennedy at his inauguration and this year for him at the White House. Who knows who else will sing or speak and gather people together on this *very spot* to once again exercise democracy as it was meant to be—for the people by the people!"

"How much of this do you want in the obit?" I asked.

171

"Every word of it," she insisted. "And add this too."

"Cheeze," I mumbled. My hand was as cramped up as hers.

"As Marian sang," Miss Volker said with a bit of swagger, "who had her back?"

"Lincoln," I answered.

"A-plus again," she said robustly. "Lincoln was right behind her, praising her because her love for this country's future was greater than this country's ugly past. Marian was a visionary. The greatest lessons in history are about people changing their minds for the better," she said with reverence. "Marian went back and changed the minds of the Daughters of the American Revolution. She did not want anger and bitterness within herself and she didn't want it in her enemies either. Lincoln too changed his mind when he realized he was not just fighting a war to beat the South but fighting for a better Union, a Union of free people joined together with common beliefs."

"What about this history lesson on forgiveness changing your mind about Spizz?" I asked, trying once more to be sensible. "Think *that* over."

"I think even history is not going to bring all those poor old Norvelt ladies back to life," she replied with certainty. Then she looked toward Lincoln as she tugged her coat up over her own slumped

172

shoulders. "Remember what they did with John Wilkes Booth?"

Even I knew Booth had been shot dead through the neck while running from a burning barn. But Miss Volker's question hung stiffly in the air like the bodies of those who helped Booth—and I knew better than to help Spizz.

There wasn't anything more to say and we both looked away. I stared toward the distant White House and wondered how the president felt each morning when he looked out his window toward Lincoln—the great man who freed the slaves, saved the Union, and lost his life.

Just then a taxi pulled into the parking lot.

"Hold that cab!" Miss Volker shouted. "We'll be right down."

As we descended the stairs, a long line of chattering girls my age, all dressed in bright overcoats and hats, stepped out of the taxi like an endless scarf being pulled from a magician's jacket sleeve. As I held the taxi door for them, I envied their laughter. Somehow Mr. Hyde hadn't found them yet.

"We should buy a car," Miss Volker announced once the girls had drifted away and we settled into the backseat.

"Where will we do that?" I asked.

She pointed into the distance. I followed the line of her finger to a billboard which read,

FOGGY BOTTOM USED CARS
Guaranteed to drive you
CLEAR across the country!

"By now Spizz has a pretty big head start," I said.

She smiled a wicked smile. "My thought exactly," she replied. "Remember, the best place to harpoon a whale is in the back."

10

In fact, from the moment the taxi dropped us off at the Foggy Bottom Used Car dealership, everything about our trip started to get more than foggy.

First, Miss Volker and I had a little problem with choosing which car to buy. I was searching the lot for a car like her old Plymouth Valiant, because I knew I could drive it. But Miss Volker's eyes widened when she spotted the car of her dreams.

"Look!" she cried out, flapping her arms as she ran toward a massively long black car and threw herself across the hood as she hugged it.

When I caught up to her I saw trouble. "Why this?" I asked.

"*This* is what we are buying," she replied with absolute certainty.

"It's really big," I remarked, trying to hint with my wide-eyed look that I was afraid of its bigness. "I think it's bigger than my dad's airplane."

"It should be big," she said grandly, and kissed the hood. "It's a hearse. You have to be able to fit a casket in the back."

"I know what it is," I said. "Mr. Huffer has one and Bunny used to have her *dead doll* tea parties in the back."

"We won't be having a tea party," she said gleefully. "This will be perfect for hauling the white whale around before we give him a proper burial."

I had to open the driver's side door with both hands. It felt like I was opening a bank vault. When I sat on the front seat I sank down so low I couldn't see over the dashboard. I felt like I was driving my own casket. The pedals were two feet farther away than what I could reach and the steering wheel was the size of a bicycle tire.

"I don't think I can drive this beast," I said out the window. "It's too *big*."

"You sound like fussy little Goldilocks," she snapped. "Now put some effort into this. Not everything in life is *just right*."

"Even if you put me on a medieval rack and stretch me into Turkish Taffy, I couldn't drive this car," I protested. "I'm too short."

The moment I said that, she began to pout as she had on the train, when those soggy beads of wet bread trailed down her face like little white garden snails. When she didn't get her way, bad things were about to happen.

That's when the car salesman came hopping toward us from his log cabin office. He had a tidy human face on the upright body of a well-dressed cat. Something must have been wrong with his fidgety legs because every few seconds he adjusted his balance as if he were standing on the tip of a pointy stick. He smiled a slender, toothy smile at Miss Volker and adjusted his skinny plaid tie.

"Hello," he purred. He was foggy too.

"Hello," Miss Volker barked back at him.

"This used hearse is a bargain," he declared, and quickly began to polish the side mirror with a colorful silk pocket square. "But it's not all used up. There are plenty more bodies it can carry around for you—or if you are a florist you can use it to make deliveries." He quickly ticked off a few more practical uses for the hearse, from "mobile day-care facility" to "extra-large pizza delivery."

"It's the perfect vehicle," agreed Miss Volker, "but *he* said we need something smaller—I guess he means something that would hold the peewee wooden coffin of a boy." She shot me a cross look.

"Pardon my manners," the salesman asked in a very svelte tone, "but what is your name, ma'am?"

"Miss Volker," she replied bluntly.

"Volker!" he sang out, suddenly perking up and rubbing his nubby feline hands together with joy. "Oh, I have just the car for you. I always match up names of cars with their owners. For instance, if your name is Dodge you buy a Dodge. If it is Ford . . ."

"Nothing by Ford," she insisted harshly. "He was anti-labor and blamed the Jews for everything bad in the world, and he didn't read books. He thought the American Revolution took place in 1812. He was mean to his family, and he was ignorant except for how to build cars."

"Clearly, you are not a Ford," he concluded, bowing and backing up as if she were royalty. "You have a more illustrious *history* running through your veins."

As soon as he said the word *history* her ears glowed and she seemed to like him more.

"I have a *Volks*wagen Beetle," he offered, and smiled confidently. "A perfect fit between woman and machine, for as you must know, *Volk* means 'folks' in German. It fits your name *perfectly*!"

He pranced us over to the bright red car and it did perfectly match our needs for a lot of reasons. Mostly, it was my "perfect fit," and as he rhapsodized about the German engineering, I quickly slipped into the front seat and held the wheel. I could easily reach the pedals, and when I turned my head to the left and right I could see out the windows.

I got out to check the engine, but when I opened the hood all I found was a luggage compartment big enough for the loose spare tire and some tools.

"The engine's in back, son," the salesman said. "Runs great, as the windshield says."

I opened the rear compartment and pretended to know something about motors as I examined the lawnmower-sized engine.

I loved the car but Miss Volker detested it.

"I know a lot of *Volks*," she said with authority, and crossed her arms, "who since World War II will not buy anything German—especially a car designed by Hitler's Nazi gang, who built tanks and other war machines!"

"Oh dear," he replied, and his entire body twisted up in anguish. "Then perhaps you have a middle name that will inspire a match—Packard perhaps? Cadillac?"

He nervously hopped around from side to side and back and forth as if the thin legs inside his pants were pogo sticks. We followed him along the rows of cars and considered a Chevy and a Rambler. Then we dragged ourselves past a Chrysler, a Pontiac, a Buick, a Mercury, and an Oldsmobile. She disliked them all.

"Do you have anything like a whaling ship on wheels?" I asked, trying to be clever because Miss Volker's face was looking as testy as Mrs. Captain Ahab's.

"Darn," exclaimed the salesman as he snapped his fingers. "I did have a spiffy Amphicar that drives on land or sea. It was bright baby-blue and as cute and tidy as a ship in a bottle. But I just sold it an hour ago to a big guy who was driving to Tennessee."

"USS *Spizz*!" she hissed like a steam vent.

"How did you know his name?" the salesman asked, fussing compulsively with his jacket buttons.

"We're heading to the same place," she replied knowingly, and circled back to the Volkswagen.

"Think of it as a German submarine," I whispered eagerly. "I'm sure we can blow him out of the water."

"Okay," she groaned reluctantly. "We better get moving. Spizz is already going over land and lakes in his vehicle. But just remember that this Kraut car is *your* decision, because it's against my moral judgment."

I reached into her purse, felt the pistol, but only removed her wallet where she kept the big bills. I counted out two hundred dollars.

The salesman recounted it while whistling a jaunty tune, and then opened his jacket. He slipped the money into one inside pocket and from the other he fished out a charm bracelet of car keys. "The VW is perfect for you, ma'am. Trust me," he said as he unfastened the key and eased it into her hand. "The war is over and the Germans are now good *Volks*."

"We'll meet you inside," she replied through clenched teeth, "after a little test drive."

"I'll prepare the paperwork," he sang merrily, and hopped away as if he were bouncing along a country path.

As soon as he was inside his cabin Miss Volker tossed me the key. "Quick," she said urgently. "Let's hit the road."

"Why?" I asked.

"Because neither of us has a license and only one of us can drive," she explained, "and *he* is underage."

She was right. I hopped into the car and reached over and opened her door and she got in. I started the engine and then I looked down at the pedals. "Cheeze," I said in dismay, "why are there three pedals?"

"It's a stick shift, ninny," she replied. "You said you could drive it!"

"I've only driven automatics," I blurted out nervously.

"Automatics!" she echoed scornfully. "You get a failing grade at being a boy. Now push in the clutch pedal and put the stick into R for reverse and step on the gas while you slowly let up on the clutch—and don't forget to release the emergency brake."

I did all of that and we jolted straight back like a dog yanked on a short leash. I slammed on the brakes and the clutch and stopped a foot before we flattened an old police motorcycle with a sidecar.

"Now put it in first gear," she instructed, "and let out the clutch."

I did, and we shot forward and I steered out of the car lot onto an empty street.

"Now second gear!" she instructed once the engine began to whine. "Now third . . . now fourth."

We took off down the road, and after a few miles I seemed to get the hang of using a clutch and shifting gears. I turned and smiled at her. "This is a great car," I remarked. "Perfect fit."

"Hitler loved *perfection*," she replied with a bit of menace in her voice. "He tortured all of humanity with his quest for *perfection*."

"Where are we going?" I asked, changing the subject and trying to get a clear view out of the windshield. RUNS GREAT! was still painted across the glass.

"Tennessee," she replied.

"It'll take a month to get there," I groaned.

"You don't know anything about geography," she said. She pointed to a gas station and when I pulled to a stop she sent me in for highway maps of Virginia and Tennessee. On the way back to the VW I saw a wrecked car by the side of the station. I hustled over to it and swiped the license plate, which was barely hanging on by a loose screw. There was some rusty wire on the ground. I picked it up and quickly secured the license plate to the back of the VW.

I had us back on the road in minutes.

"I'll teach you a few things. Now keep your eyes peeled for Highway 50 west and your foot heavy on the gas."

As I followed her directions across the Potomac River into Virginia, I was going flat out. I definitely gave myself an A+ on my driver's test. I had both hands on the wheel. I was passing cars on the left and right, and if they didn't get out of my lane I ducked way down and hit the horn with my forehead. If the horn didn't scare them, then what looked like a Headless Horseman driver and his ghostly granny sure did. If someone looked at me like I was too young to drive, I just put my arm around Miss Volker's neck, held her close and said, "Give your Spizz Junior a big kiss." Then I gave her a loud smooch. That made them look away!

Once I broke free from the pack and had no one ahead of me I reached for the radio.

"Don't turn that on!" she screeched above the noise

from the engine. "A little Nazi inside will start ordering us around in German. If you want news, just ask me. I'll be your radio."

"But you are like a radio of the past," I said. "When you open your mouth, dead people speak."

"You are mistaken," she countered. "When I open my mouth, dead people come alive with the wisdom of the ages."

"If they were so wise, how come the present, as my dad says, is worse than the past?" I asked.

"Because the military taught your father that winning a war would make life better. But war doesn't care about winners and losers. War consumes the losers on its unrelenting march to ruin the lives of the victors."

After that I kept my mouth shut and drove like a racing maniac all afternoon. I loved the thrill of highway driving and felt I could motor nonstop around the world.

After we made a pit stop for snacks and gas, Miss Volker slept. As the road started winding and rolling into the Appalachian Mountains I was getting drowsy, but suddenly Miss Volker snapped open her eyes and yelled out, "Hit the brakes!"

I did and we screeched to a stop, causing the car following behind to swerve around us. The driver honked his horn and shook his fist at us as he passed.

"What are we stopping for?" I asked. In the rear-view mirror I saw two smoking lines of burnt rubber behind us. If there had been ice on the road, we would have slid to Tennessee. "I didn't see a deer or a squirrel in the road."

"Of course not," she said. "You only see what you already know. Now back up and read that historic marker on the side of the road."

I did. "It says this is where the Proclamation Line of 1763 passed by," I said. "I never heard of it."

"Because they don't teach it in school. This is stuff you learn from reading books all your life," she explained.

"Or from listening to you," I added.

"One of these days I'll be *dead*, so you better not count on me to spoon-feed you brains forever. This Proclamation boundary," she explained, "was between Native Americans and the British Crown. It was meant to keep Colonial settlers from crossing into Indian Territory. Basically the treaty stated that all the rivers that flowed from here to the Atlantic Ocean marked the territory for the Colonists. And all the rivers that flowed from here west to the Mississippi belonged to the Indians and they could keep their land as pure as their ancestors always kept it. But the treaty didn't hold, and once again there was trouble in paradise. The moment the Colonies won independence from the British, they celebrated their new freedom by making sure the Indians lost theirs.

"Frontiersmen stepped over the line and invaded Indian lands. That caused trouble, so our new government set new treaties and then broke them, and with each broken treaty we always wanted more land and less Indians. The great Shawnee chief Tecumseh said about his people, 'They have vanished before the avarice and oppression of the white man, as snow before a summer sun.'"

I put the VW back in gear and headed west like an old-time settler. That history had already passed us by, but if I could ever go fast enough to catch it from behind, I'd change things around and give the Indians back their land.

"Even Lincoln," she said with shame in her voice, "as he fought to free African Americans from plantation slavery with one hand, he fought with the other hand to make reservation slaves of the Native Americans. His worst moment came after the Dakota War when in 1862 he had thirty-eight Sioux braves hanged in Minnesota territory—the largest one-day hanging in American history, ordered by the greatest president in American history."

"Jekyll and Hyde," I remarked, and mashed down on the gas pedal with all my strength. Now I really wished

I could catch history and give the Sioux braves back their lives too.

"Nobody is pure," she echoed. "On the white man side of the Line of Proclamation, Lincoln is a hero. On the Native American side, he is a villain."

"I didn't know that," I said.

"You do now," she replied. "And never forget this rule of U.S. history—America always loses a war it fights against itself."

We didn't talk for a while, which was good because when you learn important lessons you need time to remember them in ink.

About an hour later she shifted around in her seat like a dog getting comfortable. "Well, I figure you might be curious about the town of Rugby we're going to visit and why my family got kicked out."

I was still driving like a possessed demon chasing the setting sun over the horizon. I hadn't given Rugby any thought whatsoever, but that didn't stop her from telling me.

"Rugby began as the greatest utopian town in America, and it was started by Thomas Hughes, who wrote *Tom Brown's School Days*."

I slapped my hands on the steering wheel with excitement. "Well, I have news for you," I said triumphantly. "I'm not as stupid as I look. I own that book!"

"You mean you have the Classics Illustrated version,"

she said with contempt, making it clear that I had the moron version of the book.

"Yes," I said, staring out between the letters on the windshield. "I have it in my suitcase."

"Well, maybe I can convince you to read the real book. When Thomas Hughes was a boy he went to a private school called Rugby in England. There was a tradition in those days of older boys bullying younger boys. Hughes was bullied a lot. After he finished school, he wrote *Tom Brown's School Days,* which is all about the evils of being bullied. The book was an instant success and Hughes made oodles of money, and with it he decided to build a perfect community in the wilderness in 1880—a utopian paradise that was free of bullies and full of freethinkers. So he came to America and bought a lot of cheap land far in the hills of Tennessee and began to construct a small English village and advertise for good people to join him.

"My parents were attracted to the idea of a community where each day people would learn how to be kinder to each other, and more responsible for their own behavior. Other people felt the same too, and right away the town took off. Cottages were built for families. There was a charming Victorian inn, and a library, and farms, and workshops for canning goods, and in the evenings there was music and gatherings of all sorts—and everyone was equal.

"I remember one night as a girl I was milking a goat and my father walked into the barn. I had both hands working the goat's udder and the milk was splish-splashing into the bucket in a one-two, one-two rhythm. My father listened to that rhythm for a little while and then he just said to me, 'Milking sets the cycle of the mind. You begin life by believing what you see, and then you question it and arrive at another conclusion. Then you believe in what you concluded, and then you question that. Tick-tock, tick-tock, question-answer, question-answer, one-two, one-two. This is how you listen to yourself, or read a book, or anything else that moves your mind, until one day the clock stops and you hope your milk bucket is full of nourishing wisdom.' I always remember him saying that," she said. "What he meant was, the moment you think you know something for sure, then you darn well better question it."

"I like that too," I agreed. "If you question everything, then there is no one way to do anything."

"Exactly," she said. "Except for the church. They didn't question themselves. They only questioned everyone else." I could hear the disappointment in her voice. "Utopia for the preacher was not heaven on earth in Tennessee. Utopia could only be eternal life after death *if* you went to God's heaven. And you could only get to heaven one way, and that was through following the teaching of the Bible."

"That led to a problem, right?" I guessed.

"Big problem," she replied firmly. "Just like the Puritans in Boston. They were the same way. They left England for America to start a 'Shining City on a Hill'—a new world of religious purity—but look out if you questioned any of their religious beliefs. They hanged witches, impure thinkers, and non-Puritans on the Boston Commons as a warning to freethinkers. Anne Hutchinson was a freethinking Puritan, a woman who dared to believe that she could pray directly to God and receive His grace without the need of a preacher. Well, the Puritan church did not want that kind of freethinking. After they hanged Anne's Quaker friend Mary Dyer, they chased Anne out of town. She fled to Providence but then heard the Puritans were still after her so she went farther south into the Dutch territory—to a place called Split Rock just above New York."

"This isn't going to have a happy ending, is it?" I asked.

"Nope," she said grimly. "Anne Hutchinson and her family were scalped and killed by Indians who were already angry with settlers for taking their land."

"Trouble in paradise," I said.

"Jekyll and Hyde," she echoed. "But she would have still been living safely in Boston if the Puritans had allowed for freedom of religion and had not driven her into hostile territory."

I pulled around a truck full of turkeys stacked in wire pens. They were headed for the wrong side of Thanksgiving dinner.

"So what happened to your family?" I asked.

"Funny you should ask," she replied.

"But it's not funny, right?" I guessed.

"Right," she said. "My father was a big tick-tock thinker and he liked Thomas Jefferson. Jefferson's vision for America was farmland for everyone to grow their own food. Everyone could be self-sufficient in communities of good people where everyone helped each other. Another thing my father liked about Jefferson was that Jefferson secretly made his own Bible. When Jefferson read the Bible he was more interested in what Jesus said about how to live, and how people should treat one another, and about love and humanity and good deeds and kindness. Jefferson was not so interested in what others said *about* Jesus—which made up most of the Bible. So he cut out the parts of the Bible where Jesus said something important and pasted them together to make his own secret Bible. It had to be a secret because Christians were still very much like the Puritans—they accepted only one Bible. Making your own Bible was frowned upon, even punished.

"Well, my father did the same thing as Jefferson, but somehow his Bible was found and it made a lot of people upset. Like me, he was a big talker, and he was probably talking loudly about it and one thing led to another, and after a lot of church debates about who believed what, we were asked to leave. And we did. It was like my parents were Adam and Eve and my sister and I were their sinful kids and we were kicked out of Eden. But I never forgot Rugby because it is Eden in my memory. The truth is, Rugby didn't last long after we left. There was a terrible typhoid outbreak in the beginning, a bad fire, and arguments over land ownership that made neighbors enemies. As more original settlers left, it became a ghost town, but it is forever the home of my childhood and that's why I'm looking forward to going again. I want to visit in honor of my sister and the happy time we had there together. And Spizz will be there. I know he will. He loved Rugby."

"Why was he kicked out?"

"He wasn't. He always followed the rules. Remember what a pest he was in Norvelt? Giving people tickets for having weeds in their yard and stopped-up gutters. Spizz was perfect for Rugby because he didn't question anything. For him, there was no such thing as a bad rule, and when he follows the rules he is a very happy man. He only ran away from Rugby because he loved me. He followed our family around like a dog and lived in all the towns I lived in with my parents. He'd rent rooms and have sketchy jobs as a handyman and bother me, and eventually when I got the nursing job in Norvelt he moved there too. He thought we'd get married."

"Now that you mention marriage, there was something I didn't tell you," I said sheepishly, not wanting to get her worked up. "On the train, when Spizz cornered me in the bathroom, he said he had returned to Norvelt the night Mrs. Custard died because the two of you were planning to run off and get married. He said you agreed to marry him because you lost the bet and were the last old lady standing in Norvelt."

"He's hallucinating," she protested. "*He* returned to kill Mrs. Custard because he's an insane old-lady serial killer."

"I'm just telling you what he told me," I stated. Then I took my life in my own hands when I added, "And he told me you killed Mrs. Custard because you wanted to be the last old-lady Norvelter so *you* could marry *him*."

"Now I'm really determined to kill that liar," she vowed. "He's worse than I thought."

"And you are sure he'll be at Rugby?" I asked.

"Positively," she said with vengeful confidence. "He

always shows up wherever I go. I can't shake him. That's why I have to bury him."

"So are you Jekyll and he is Hyde? Or is it the other way around?" I inquired.

She crossed her arms and gave me a stern look.

"And what about Huffer?" I asked. "I think I may have seen him get off the train in D.C. with a casket. I was going to go ask him what he was doing when you fell and fired off the shot."

"He may have been changing trains," she guessed. "He told me on the phone he's traveling down by rail. He's probably in a hurry to get to Florida so he can fix up my sister for her memorial service and pick up a check. But he has plenty of time to get there now, because when we get to Rugby I'm going to set a trap for Spizz and it will begin with you digging a single grave."

I kept driving.

11

When you slowly dig a grave in hard dirt with a shovel, you have a lot of time to think, and the first thought I had as I threw dirt over my shoulder was that the farther Miss Volker and I traveled from Norvelt the less Norvelt-like we had become. But how could I know what defined us now? I had never been away from home for a week without a parent, and I certainly had never been part of a plan to kill someone. Norvelt was a "helping hand" town, with neighbor helping neighbor, but if planning a murder was a test of my Norvelt values, I had failed. I was "helping out" but in the wrong way. I know my mother asked Miss Volker to tutor me in history and she was doing a great job on that subject, but when it came to being a good Norvelt citizen, my own mother would have given me a failing grade.

Since leaving Washington, D.C., I had been driving on skinny back roads like a bug-eyed maniac for two days on the way to Miss Volker's old hometown. At night I never got any rest, because we stayed in run-down roadside motels where I let her have the moldy-smelling rooms, while I slept out in the Beetle like a dog, all curled up with a blanket on the small backseat.

When it came to eating, I realized why my mother grew garden produce and sent nourishing dinners down to Miss Volker. She only liked to eat bags of chocolate chip cookies, ice-cream sandwiches, popcorn, and boxes of oyster crackers and salty pretzels, which she washed down with quart after quart of buttermilk.

We were in a hurry to get to Rugby, so she wouldn't stop and let me have a sit-down meal. I hadn't had any green vegetables for days. In fact, I was lucky to find a green hot dog or a furry sandwich at a gas station snack stand, so I ended up eating the same junk Miss Volker ate. My stomach felt like a vending machine.

By the time we arrived in Rugby, late in the afternoon of the third day, I was hungry, exhausted, and slumped over the steering wheel. I was eager for a clean bed, a good meal, and a pay phone so I could call home. But when we arrived at the center of town I knew those wishes were hopeless dreams.

"This is Rugby," she announced grandly as she gestured toward an overgrown weed-tangled dirt street that was lined with boarded-up wooden buildings. Everywhere I looked—north, south, east, and west—Rugby was an abandoned ghost town that time forgot.

"This is the Eden on earth where Spizz and I were born, and played together as kids, and where we learned Esperanto—the international language of peace. At one time this town was even greater than Norvelt, but it died out, and now this is where Spizz will come to be buried."

I had barely turned off the engine and staggered out of the car to stretch my aching legs and sore back when she led me to a graveyard behind what was left of the buckled walls of a decaying church.

"See," she said, pointing past the toppled steeple toward a row of graves at the far edge of the cemetery. "On that wide stone are carved the names of Spizz's parents. And the empty plot next to theirs belongs to him."

Off to the side was a weathered old shovel stuck nose-down in a pile of dirt. It looked just like the one Dad gave me to dig the Norvelt bomb shelter.

"The way you catch a murderer," she said in the hushed voice a sportsman might use while tracking wild game, "is to dig him an irresistibly *comfortable* grave."

"This is a bad idea," I said. "And it makes me *uncomfortable*."

"It's only a bad idea for someone who can't see a good idea. Now do as you are told and that will make me *comfortable*."

I tried to change the subject. "Where are your parents buried?" I asked.

"Certainly not here," she crowed, and puffed out her chest. "Once we were kicked out of paradise, we never returned."

And then she got a busy look on her face and began to walk off.

"Wait!" I called after her. "Where are you going?"

"To put together a plan to catch the Norvelt killer," she replied over her shoulder. "To do that I need some supplies, and maybe while I'm digging around I'll uncover some memento to put into my sister's casket. She loved it here. Plus, I need to find my old harpoon."

"A real harpoon?" I asked. "We are landlocked out here."

"The Rugby blacksmith made one for me," she answered. "He had been a blacksmith on Nantucket whaling ships till he got old and tired of being bounced around on the ocean. He joined Rugby to live out his life on a farm. He'd gather us kids up and tell salty yarns about whaling on the high seas. I begged him to forge me a harpoon, and he did. It was beautiful and deadly. I used to throw it at logs. Even then Spizz annoyed me. Once, I hurled it at him so hard it got stuck in a tree. Maybe it's still there."

"If you find a pay phone," I said without much hope, "let me know so I can call my mom."

"There is no phone out here," she replied. "Not even phone lines. If you suddenly died and were buried out here, nobody would find you but the worms in the ground. Now start digging—that grave has to be six feet deep to be legal. I'll be back in an hour or two."

Then she tramped off through the weeds and brush.

And so I grabbed the shovel and started digging a legal grave for an illegal death. To tell you the truth, I felt a little sorry for Spizz, because what she and I were planning to do to him was worse than what he wanted to do to us.

But I followed Miss Volker's orders, as my mother told me to do. I kept digging and digging as the sun kept sinking, and before too long it was dark. But one thing about digging a grave was that all you had to do was put the shovel in the earth, push it down with your foot, lift the dirt, and throw it out of the hole. You didn't need light for that, although the stars were dazzling and the moon was so full and bright that I still had a shadow.

And then it got creepy. Not because of graveyard ghosts, but because of the living.

"Gantos boy," somebody whispered from the thick

brush twenty feet away, almost loudly enough for me to feel his breath on the back of my neck. "Who are you digging that grave for? Yourself?"

"Cheeze-us-crust!" I shouted, and jumped straight up out of the hole. I knew it was Spizz. He was here, just as Miss Volker had predicted, but he had still surprised me.

"I figure," he said, "that she'll want to kill you like she killed all the others."

"I'm digging it for you!" I replied, looking into a clump of dark bushes that seemed to shimmer under the moonlight. "She's going to bury you right here. Next to your parents." For emphasis I shoveled a little dirt in his direction.

"Fat chance," he replied. "She wants to marry me, not kill me."

"Believe me," I said to the spot where I figured he was hiding. "She wants to kill you. You heard her take a shot at you at the train station."

"She's got terrible aim now, with those claw hands," he said with a guffaw. "So bad she missed a roomful of innocent bystanders."

"I shouldn't be telling you this," I confided in a lower voice, "but just so you know I mean you no harm, I asked her to throw away the gun. But she said she needed it for you—so you better watch out."

"Kid," he said, "you were the one standing knee-deep in an open grave. If you ask me, you are the one who needs to watch out!"

"I doubt that," I said.

"Be careful," he warned. "She's fickle. One day she loves you and the next she wants to bury you."

"Well, if I'm going to die, let me ask you a few questions," I said, feeling pretty sure Miss Volker was not going to kill me.

"Fire away!" he said, and chuckled at himself.

"What did you say about Mr. Huffer in your Esperanto note?" I asked.

"I told her that Huffer was on the train and couldn't be trusted."

"What's that mean?"

"He's trying to soak up all the reward money."

"From dead people?"

"From their families, and the police," he said. "To tell you the honest truth, Huffer's wife went door-to-door in Norvelt selling those no-good life insurance policies to dotty old ladies who didn't know better. Huffer put her in a disguise so she looked like a religious worker from the Lutheran Brotherhood Insurance Company of West Virginia. My guess is that Huffer is behind the whole scam."

"Do you have any proof?" I asked.

"Nope," he replied with regret. "But I bet he killed the policyholders after milking them for their payments, so he wouldn't have to cough up the death benefits. All I can say for sure is that Huffer is a greedy-guts for money."

"But what does this have to do with Miss Volker?" I asked.

"Huffer was the one who originally blamed the murders on Miss Volker. That's why I fled from Norvelt, so I'd look guilty and the police would leave her alone."

"So you're telling me you believe Mr. Huffer did it?" I asked, just trying to get the facts straight.

"Well, the whole Huffer family is in on it, as far as I can tell," he said, getting worked up. "And they killed Mrs. Custard too."

"Not Bunny!" I exclaimed.

"I don't know," he growled. "I don't trust her. Anyone that stumpy is evil."

"It couldn't be Bunny," I lamented.

"Well, she's the reason they need all that money," he said. "For her operation."

"What operation?"

"It's a secret," he replied. "They want to make her tall. I heard they were going to use body parts from the funeral home to make her bigger—like give her someone's arms and legs instead of those tiny doll limbs she has now."

"That's like Frankenstein!" I exclaimed. "That's insane."

"I'm just telling you what people are talking about back in Norvelt," he said.

"I think you are pulling *my* leg," I concluded. "Because it's not adding up. I'm sure Mr. Greene wouldn't print these kinds of rumors in his newspaper."

"I'll just say this one last thing," said Spizz. "That Huffer is a monster. If he could prove that Miss Volker murdered the old gals, he'd have her sent to prison, but since I already confessed, all he has to do is knock me off and collect the reward. That makes *me* the logical choice to be buried in that grave you are digging."

"But this is Miss Volker's grave for you. Why does she want you dead?"

"Something stupid," he replied, sounding contrite. "I told her I was jealous of you and if she didn't stop seeing you all the time I was going to bury you in a place where you'd never be found."

"You weren't stupid enough to tell her you'd bury me in Rugby?" I asked.

"Maybe," he said sheepishly.

"You shouldn't have done that," I said, "because now she's planning to turn the tables and bury *you* in Rugby."

"She's a vengeful lady," he said matter-of-factly. "It's part of her charm."

"I don't believe that," I said, and I was ready to say more when suddenly another man's voice hollered out from the woods at the other side of the graveyard.

"I don't believe it either!" the man said, muffling his voice like my bathroom visitor on the train. "None of it is true!"

"You're the second detective!" I said, surprised to have him show up. "What are you doing here?"

"I'm here to bring some truth to this burial party," he said. "This is what really happened."

"That's not a detective," Spizz hollered out. "That's just Huffer. He's always playing like he's a big shot."

"Mr. Huffer?" I asked the bushes. "Was it really you who tricked me on the train and tried to scare me into helping you?"

"I was just using a disguise in order to get to the bottom of the truth," he said, defending himself. "No harm done in seeking justice."

"I thought you were just trying to get to the *bottom* of the reward money," I countered.

"I'm telling you what I've known all along," he said in his normal voice. "Volker killed those old ladies. Lovesick Spizz just wants to save her for himself by telling everyone I did it. But she is the real murderer. Look at the facts. She had poison. She had reason. The police said her medical reports were false. All the evidence points to her. And Spizz's tall tale that I need money to turn my sweet little daughter into some sort of Frankenstein freak is just sick!"

I wasn't so sure about that. I had read the Classics Illustrated *Frankenstein* and the operation worked.

Suddenly the big round headlights of the Volkswagen popped on and shone brightly across the graveyard.

"I'll tell you what is sick!" Miss Volker cried out. "Neither of you can tell the truth!"

She was standing between the headlights, and even though I squinted I couldn't see her clearly, but her voice was present.

"I know *I* didn't do it," she thundered. "Huffer might be too stupid to do it, and Spizz might be too afraid of getting caught. But one of you could be just a little bit too greedy, or a little bit too much in love. Let's find out who that might be!"

Just then she stepped in front of the light. She had the pistol in one hand and what had to be her old harpoon in the other. "In case you are wondering," she said, looking back and forth to where both men were hunkered down in darkness, "I already heated up my hands over a campfire. And now that they are hot I have a chance to use them. So it's time for Mrs. Captain Ahab to clear up this fishy business."

I stepped away from the grave. My heart was

pounding and suddenly I felt my nose gushing. "Miss Volker," I said as calmly as I could. "This is not a good idea. Let's sleep on it and figure it out tomorrow."

"There will be no tomorrow for someone. Take cover in the grave," she ordered.

Suddenly Huffer hollered out to me. "Don't drop down into that hole," he advised, "or she'll bury you alive."

Spizz shouted at Miss Volker. "Careful! You might kill your little boyfriend. Though he already looks like a dead zombie with that blood smeared all over his front."

I followed Miss Volker's orders and jumped back into the grave.

"Killing Jack would break both your hearts," Miss Volker said sarcastically, "because either of you'd like to kill him yourselves."

Then with sudden swiftness she reared back with the harpoon in her hand. "White whale!" she declared in her raw Mrs. Captain Ahab voice. "Prepare to die!"

The next thing I knew, the harpoon went whistling over my head toward the bushes where I knew Spizz had been hiding in the dark.

The harpoon hit something heavy with a solid *thunk*, and I heard branches snapping.

"Close!" Spizz shouted gleefully. "But you missed me again!" Then he started to laugh. "You hit a tree, just like the last time you threw that toy at me."

"That harpoon is no toy," she said. "The blade is still long and true and sharp, and it went deep into the heart of that old tree and killed it. And you'll be dead too when it passes through your miserable blubber. I won't *miss* you next time," she promised.

"But Huffer is the killer!" Spizz replied, defending himself. "*He* dressed up like me and gave the poison cookie to Mrs. Custard. The only reason I returned to Norvelt was to propose to you."

"Lies!" Huffer shouted. "All lies."

But were they? I did remember Bunny saying her father used his cadaver makeup kit to reconstruct faces—and he could have made himself look like Spizz. And Mrs. Custard did say the man who gave her the cookie looked like a bigger version of me—but since I was dressed as Spizz Junior, the real Spizz could have given her the cookie. I didn't know who was telling the truth.

Miss Volker pointed the gun toward Spizz's voice. "I've got a barrelful of lead harpoons in here," she said. "Prepare to die."

"Too late!" Huffer shouted. "The killer is running away from the truth."

For a moment we all stopped talking. We could hear Spizz rustling through the bushes and trees as he retreated through the dark. He must have fallen a few times, I guessed, from his little cries and stumbling crashes. Eventually he reached his Amphicar and started the engine and *putt-putted* away.

"Sounds like that car-yacht is casting off for other shores," Miss Volker remarked, then swiftly she turned in the other direction. "Huffer, step out into the light like a man so I can shoot you."

"I didn't hurt anyone," he said boldly from his hiding spot.

"I can't take that chance," she said. "Both you and Spizz should be buried in that one grave."

"Hear that, Jack?" Huffer said. "She wants both Spizz and me dead so she can avoid blame. With us gone she'll have gotten away with murder *and* she'll get the reward."

Miss Volker raised her arm and pointed the gun straight and aimed at the voice. "I should shoot you just because you bought the hearse I wanted at Foggy Bottom Used Cars," she said with contempt. "I saw where you parked it down the road here. I knew it was yours because of the window-view casket in the back you are going to put my sister in."

"I could put you in it if you'd like," he dared to say. "After all, you'll get the electric chair for murder."

"Keep talking," she said, adjusting her aim. "I think I can just see the whites of your terrified eyes."

"Actually," he said, "I think you should look a little closer." Suddenly he stepped out from behind a bush and into the beam of light from the Beetle. "I'd tell you to pull the trigger," he said calmly as he stepped toward her, "but by my watch your hands have frozen up again. As usual, your mouth was going a mile a minute and time passed you by." He walked deliberately at the barrel of the gun.

From my viewpoint, he was a dark shadow of a man with his black overcoat, black suit, black shoes, black gloves, and coal-black hat.

"Don't take another step forward," she warned him.

He did, and then he took another.

"Your fingers," he said knowingly, "feeling stiff, are they?" He spread out his arms and presented his full chest as a target. "Take your best shot."

The gun was shaking in her hand. Her jaw was clenched. Her legs stood firm. But even though her fingers were as curled as fishhooks, they would not curl far enough to catch the trigger inside the finger guard.

Then Huffer lowered his arms and casually ambled right up to the gun until the barrel poked him in the chest.

"Ha!" he spat. Then, for a stocky man, he swiftly reached out with his gloved hand and snatched the pistol from her frozen grip. "Thanks," he said. "I guess you didn't have it in you to kill one more person."

"I didn't kill anyone," she growled.

"Your fingerprints are still on the gun," he said. "Just the evidence the police will need when they find Spizz shot dead and the gun by his side. So if you go to the police you'll be doing me a favor—I'll have killed two birds with one stone."

"I'll strangle you with my own hands," she said coldly.

"But you can't," he said with false sadness. "So just let this happen. It will be better for you if he takes the fall. He was dumb enough to confess, so he's dumb enough to die. You'll get away with murder, and once I take care of him and get the reward, then we can take care of your sister. So no funny business until we meet again in Florida. Keep in mind that casket is big enough for two."

Then he drifted into the night until he blended in with the darkness.

In a minute we heard the engine of the hearse backfire a few times before it finally started up and sent dirt and gravel spraying out from under the tires as he drove away.

"We've got to get that gun back!" she said. "You heard him. If he shoots Spizz through the heart it will be like shooting me in the back."

I stuck my shovel in the dirt.

"We can't do anything at the moment," I said, stepping out of the grave. "Let's figure this out in the morning. There is nothing like a good night's sleep before solving a murder."

I walked up to her and took her hard hand and

warmed it in mine. "If you sleep in your old house, I'll sleep in the car again," I suggested.

"My house is long gone, but our beds are waiting for us around the corner in the old Hughes library," she said grandly. "It's one of the few early buildings still in good shape. I think some old-time book lovers from the area have been looking after it. As kids we called it the Rip Van Winkle library because everyone fell asleep in those big overstuffed chairs—even me."

"I read *Rip Van Winkle*," I said.

"I'm sure you read the idiot's version," she replied.

I had. I reached into the car and turned off the lights so the battery wouldn't wear down. Then I caught up to her.

"You know," she said, reflecting on her thoughts as she spoke, "I never trusted Huffer. Dealing in death all day can kill a person's love of life."

I still wasn't sure who to trust. She threw that harpoon like she wanted to deep-six Spizz. And if she could have tightened her finger a quarter of an inch she would have blown Huffer head-over-heels into the grave and I'd have to bury him.

I didn't know who did what, but like Rip Van Winkle, I was ready to sleep for twenty years and wake up long after they figured it out on their own.

12

Maybe I did sleep for twenty years because it was pitch-black when I curled up on that overstuffed chair, but when I woke up the darkness had been replaced with packed floor-to-ceiling shelves of brightly colored books. I was still in the same chair but it was as if I had fallen asleep like a caveman and woken up as a librarian.

The sun shone in through the gothic windows and the gold ink stamped on the cloth spines lit up like electric filaments. The small room glowed with titles of nineteenth-century books. It didn't matter that they were forgotten for so long. They could sleep for a thousand years and wake up on the same page where they nodded off.

I stiffly swung my legs to one side and stood up on

my feet. I took a few unsteady steps toward a wall of shelves. I reached out to touch a book but the moment I saw my hand moving, the library spell was broken and I thought of Miss Volker. I quickly spun around, but she was gone. I didn't like it when I couldn't see her. Mom had told me to keep an eye on Miss Volker at all times, which was good advice because the moment I turned my back, something bad always happened.

I went outside. It was early and the sun was just above the hills. Not far away she had a little fire going in a rusty bucket and was slowly swaying from side to side as she passed her hands over the flames.

"When I was a younger woman and Norvelt was just starting out," she said, flinching from the heat and kicking at the dirt, "I felt like I had a choice to make. It was 1934 and the country was in the middle of the Depression. People were dead broke. They either had to stick together and help each other out, or stick up banks and just help themselves. Well, a lot of people decided to rob banks, like Baby Face Nelson, John Dillinger, and Pretty Boy Floyd. I followed their doomed lives in the newspapers. But the bandit I wanted to be most was Bonnie Parker," she said wistfully.

"She and her boyfriend, Clyde, led a wild life on the run while raising Cain and robbing banks. They were heartless criminals. I knew they were awful but at the time, when so many people were out of work, and with the banks kicking people out of their homes, Bonnie and Clyde seemed heroic. We all cheered each time they knocked off a bank. 'That's one for the little people!' we'd shout.

"I guess I was a bit more romantic back then, because sometimes I imagined myself as a gun moll and I really wanted Spizz to sweep me off my feet like Clyde did with Bonnie. I wanted to smoke cigars and pack a pistol and thumb my nose at the law and all the rich bigwigs who had run the country into the ground—or at least I thought I did when I was on one of my rebellious *streaks*."

I had read all about Bonnie and Clyde and knew things didn't turn out well for them. After a long killing spree, they were driving toward a hideout in Louisiana when the police ambushed them and fired about a hundred special steel bullets that perforated one side of the car, passed clean through Bonnie and Clyde, and out the other side of the car. They never saw the ambush *coming*—and they didn't have time to feel themselves *going*.

Once the cops pulled Bonnie and Clyde's bodies out of the getaway car, they put the shot-up corpses on display. For miles around, all sorts of people who had been cheering for Bonnie and Clyde gathered to have their picture taken with the grisly-looking remains. Souvenir hunters cut off locks of Bonnie's hair and sold pieces of her bloody dress. Someone even tried to cut off Clyde's trigger finger.

"I wish I had a cigar to smoke right now," Miss Volker said as smoke from her bucket fire swirled around her heated hands.

I almost suggested that she just snap off a finger and smoke that.

"Yep, I'm feeling a little bit like I did in the old days, when I was full of vinegar and no man could hold me down—especially that old stick-in-the-mud Spizz. He is a pathetic creature—a man without an imagination. All he had to do back then was show some get-up-and-go and reveal a swashbuckling side, and maybe then I would have run off with him. But instead he kept boring me with his ho-hum wooing, which did me double the harm because it chased off any other man who showed an interest in me. Then, soon after Bonnie and Clyde were gunned down, I made the sensible decision to settle down and become the nurse for Norvelt."

"I'm glad you did," I said. "Because it seems like 1934 was a very bad year to be an outlaw."

"Well, looking back on my life, I'm glad I spent a chunk of it in Norvelt. It has great meaning for me to have helped other people. But nothing lasts forever. The Puritans thought they would be pure forever. The

Indians thought their forests would last forever. The South thought slavery would last forever. Horse breeders thought the horse and buggy would last forever. Engineers thought the steam locomotive would last forever. Even Rugby thought it would last forever.

"But life moves on, and as the preacher here used to say when he wanted us to plow the land and tend the cows, 'God helps those who help themselves.' And now I think I'll finally listen to him, because I'm ready to help myself and make up for lost time. I've already been Dr. Jekyll and lived the good utopian life at Norvelt, and now it's time to let Mr. Hyde live that other kind of utopian life—the life of doing anything you dang well please."

The smoke from the fire swirled around her as if the nice Dr. Jekyll was burning up and the swarthy Mr. Hyde was about to emerge from her soul and transform her into an evil killer.

"How can doing anything you want be utopian?" I asked. "You have to have some rules."

She gave me a disagreeable look. "You sound just like Spizz. Bonnie and Clyde did whatever they wanted to do without the burden of thinking of the consequences. They loved each other and did what they wanted—right up until the very second they died."

"Which made for a very short utopia," I remarked.

"Well put," she granted. "When you are young, doing whatever awful stuff you feel like doing never seems to last long enough. Then, when you grow up and mature, you try to make the world a better place. But when you grow old you'll find that you get a second chance at being young and restless again. You can do anything wild you want, and instead of being shot down by the police you just wander off into the wilderness like a wily old cat and are never seen again."

"Then we better not waste any more of your valuable utopian time," I said, nodding toward the car. "Because I don't want to be responsible when you wander off into the wilderness and I have to track you down. Right now we have a long drive ahead of us."

"You're right," she agreed. "The sooner we get to the fountain of youth in Saint Augustine, the sooner I'll be able to kick up my heels—and when we get to Miami I'll be able to raise some Cain of my own."

We didn't have much to pack. I strapped our two small suitcases onto the luggage rack. She had found a thin bridle rope for the harpoon, which she sent me into the woods by the graveyard to find. After I'd yanked it from a tree trunk, she showed me how to knot the rope through the bottom hole in the harpoon's shaft. I secured her weapon onto the roof rack as well, and then I knotted the other end of the rope to the front bumper.

A few minutes later, we were ready to pull out of Rugby like Bonnie and Clyde after knocking over the entire town.

Miss Volker had her window open and the smoking bucket with a few hot coals on the floor between her legs. She had made me load up the backseat with small pieces of wood to keep the fire going.

"I want my hands warm and ready for criminal action," she announced firmly, and wiggled her fingers in my face. "If I had kept them heated up last night, I wouldn't have had my pistol ripped out of my hands."

"Which turns out to be a good thing," I pointed out.

"But Mrs. Captain Ahab still has her harpoon," she said wickedly. "And it is a mighty weapon in the hands of an old salt like me."

"Just keep missing your target," I advised. "I think last night's history showed that it is better to scare your enemy away rather than dig a hole to bury him in."

"Last night is behind us and we have the whole seven seas to explore. Now raise the sails," she ordered. "Keep the wind at your back, and your eyes open for the white whale."

I put the car in gear and we pulled out of Rugby. I had to follow her instructions because she claimed she had a shortcut to save us time.

About an hour later, after we had taken some dirt

roads that looked like cow paths, our sails were pretty limp and we were back where we started. I asked if she knew where we were going.

"When I was here last," she said, "we just followed the birds."

"Well, we need a local map," I said. "Or a compass. Something to give us directions. I don't think the birds follow the roads."

We kept poking along and sailing in one circle after another until Miss Volker hollered out, "Land ho!"

Down the dusty road was a country store with a gas pump and we pulled in. I went into the store and looked around. A man as old as the cracker barrel he sat on asked if he could help me.

I told him where we were going and that we needed a map.

"Funny you should tell me this," he said in a long, slow voice. "An undertakin' fella in a big ol' hearse came in here backfiring and clanking with car trouble. He was looking for a map and a mechanic. I called a tow truck for him and he got hauled away just about an hour ago."

That had to be Huffer, I thought. "Did you get him a map too?" I asked.

"Nope," he replied. "Don't have a map and don't need one. Let me see your hand—palm up."

I stuck it out and he studied it with one eye screwed

shut, squinting down at my palm as if it were a treasure map.

"Take your life line here for about a mile," he instructed. "And at your bad-luck line take a left, then a right onto your money line, and a right where this love line merges with your disaster line, and you'll find hard pavement."

"Really?" I questioned.

"Whatever you do," he warned, "don't follow the marriage line. The bridge is out."

I didn't know what to say to that but I was starving, so I filled a paper bag with beef jerky sticks and cheese. When Miss Volker arrived I steered her into a corner where she could pick out some cookies, and I whispered to her what the clerk told me about Mr. Huffer.

"Good," she said quietly, and smiled. "We need to get to Miami before him."

"Why?" I asked.

"He's got the gun," she said wisely. "I'd rather be waiting for him than have him waiting for me."

I paid for our breakfast snacks and a six-pack of root beer for Miss Volker. Then, as we were walking out the door she saw some buckets of old house paint.

"How much for the paint?" she hollered.

"If you buy a brush, you get the paint for free," he said. "It's only twenty years old."

"Grab two wild colors," she said, "quick!"

"Why?" I asked, and picked up a bucket of bright green with one hand and something that looked like orange vomit with the other.

"You've never been on the run before, have you?" she asked. "We need to disguise ourselves from those who might do us harm."

I borrowed a screwdriver from the store clerk and opened the can of green. I dipped the wide brush in and began to paint the car from the top down. I slathered too much on, and it dripped over the headlights and down the windshield. When I wiped it off the windshield some of the "RUNS GREAT" lettering chipped away. I used the screwdriver to scrape off some more but stopped when I saw I was scratching the glass.

"Cheap German car!" Miss Volker remarked, but before she could go on a tirade she spotted a pay phone on the side of the building. "I'm going to call Mr. Hap and make plans for when we get to Miami," she said.

When she returned, I had cleaned up the headlights and pretty much painted everything else green.

She looked at the car and made a funny face. "That is not the color I would choose if I was trying to hide from a posse," she said.

"They'll think we are a couple of clowns," I replied from over my shoulder as I walked to the pay phone. I dialed the operator and placed a collect call home. Mom picked up on the second ring.

"Hello?" she said.

"I have a collect call for Mrs. Betty Gantos. Is she there to accept the charges?" the operator asked. "Her son is on the line."

"She's out delivering meals to the elderly," Mom said loudly as she talked a mile a minute, "and after that she is working the tag sale at the Community Center and after that she is ironing the uniforms for the volunteer firemen and after that she is—"

"Okay, I get it," the operator snapped back, and paused long enough to take a long drag on a cigarette, "she's not home."

"Correct," Mom replied. "And Mr. Gantos is flying to—"

The operator cut her off. "Your mother is a busybody," she said to me. "And I understand why your dad flew the coop." Then she hung up, and I ambled back to the car wondering where Dad had gone.

Once we started driving I followed the imaginary map directions on my hand until we merged onto a paved road just as the store clerk said. On the corner was a service station. Huffer's hearse was parked in front. The hood was up. A mechanic was leaning over one fender with a wrench and Huffer was leaning over the other with his black hat in his hand. I beep-beeped the horn and Miss Volker and I waved. Huffer looked up but he only saw the back of our car.

We had a long drive ahead of us, so I floored the VW and we were going so fast the wet paint was rippling up on the hood and creeping onto the windshield. I tried to turn on the windshield wipers but they were broken.

We drove south for a couple hours when I noticed a police motorcycle with a sidecar heading toward us. It looked just like the beat-up one I had almost flattened at the Foggy Bottom Used Cars lot. And suddenly I realized the driver was the little ferret-faced detective, who probably overshot the road to Rugby and was trying to find his way back.

Miss Volker saw him too and didn't seem to be surprised as he approached. "Figures that rodent detective would drive a cop cycle," she remarked. "Stay far to the left and make sure he passes on my side. I have a bone to pick with him. He almost collared Spizz and denied me the pleasure of getting him myself."

"Why can't we just duck when he passes by?" I shouted. "He won't recognize us in our disguised car."

"Damn the torpedoes," she replied, "and full speed ahead."

"Admiral Farragut said that at the Battle of Mobile Bay," I added.

"A-plus!" she hollered, then leaned out the window

and with her warmed hands undid my slip knot and grabbed the harpoon off the roof rack.

When the detective saw the harpoon in her hand, he reached into his jacket pocket and pulled out a small pistol and aimed it at the car. We were under attack!

When he was about twenty feet away, Miss Volker cawed out in her Mrs. Captain Ahab voice, "Stay away from the white whale!" And before the detective could answer or pull the trigger, she cocked her arm back and prepared to chuck the harpoon at him. A look of ferret panic widened his eyes, and as he jerked his gun hand up to protect his face he dropped the pistol. It hit the sidecar and bounced off and went end over end until it skittered across the road. His other hand pulled the handlebars to the side and he swerved toward a line of trees.

"Man overboard!" Miss Volker shouted as she wedged the harpoon between her seat and the door with the vicious point sticking out the window. "Hope he can swim to shore before the sharks get him. Ha!"

I looked into the rearview mirror. He had regained control of his motorcycle and had stopped and was looking on the ground for his gun. If I was him, I wouldn't be very happy about what had just happened.

"You better reload that harpoon," I advised her. "He had a gun."

"But he didn't have the guts to use it," she said, and

stirred up her bucket embers, filling the car with smoke. "But if he gets close again, I'll puncture him right in his cleft chin."

I coughed, wiped my nose on my sleeve, and hit the gas and we kept speeding down the road until he was a dark speck in my rearview mirror, and then he was out of sight.

We drove for a good long while at top speed. I kept checking the rearview mirror, but the detective was nowhere to be seen.

"Pull over at the first gas station you see," Miss Volker said. "All that excitement has excited my bladder."

"Me too," I agreed.

I passed one that looked pretty seedy but soon found one that was new. I pulled in and she hopped out to go around back to the restroom. I asked the attendant to top off the gas tank. If he noticed I was an underage driver, he didn't say a word. I think he may have been distracted by the state of our car, and the harpoon.

"You folks seem to be on a mission," he said.

"How did you know?" I asked.

"Just a guess," he said. "Why don't you let me check your oil and take care of that windshield for you? I have some solvent that will clean it right up."

I thanked him and went inside for more food and drinks. I also spotted a map of the southeastern states and picked that up. When the attendant returned, we settled up, and then I saw a stack of pamphlets for tourist destinations next to the cash register.

One of them was for the Roosevelts' Little White House in Warm Springs, Georgia. Wow, I thought, Miss Volker will love this.

Once she returned to the car, I went to the restroom. When I hustled back I showed her the pamphlet. "Do you want to go?" I asked. "It's perfect for us." With our clean windshield I didn't have to hunch and squint so much and I felt ready to drive forever.

"Let's skip Warm Springs," she said, sounding a bit defeated. "That Little White House just depresses me. It depressed Eleanor too, because that is where Franklin died, and when he died he was with his girlfriend."

"The president had a girlfriend?" I exclaimed. "But he was married."

"And unfaithful," she said sadly. "One day Eleanor was going through Franklin's luggage and found love letters from the other woman, Lucy Mercer. It hurt Eleanor's feelings terribly, but she didn't want to rock the boat and ruin his political career, so she suffered in silence. Franklin knew he was wrong but he chose to give in to his pleasure while ignoring her pain.

"FDR may have been our hardworking president during the Depression and our fearless commander in

226

chief during the war, but in his own home he was just a common two-timer who stabbed his wife in the back."

I figured this was why Miss Volker could never really be like Bonnie Parker and rob banks and shoot strangers, because she cared too much about other people's feelings—except Spizz's.

"We should write this girlfriend story into Eleanor's obituary," I suggested. "That's pretty important history."

"No," she replied. "That is Eleanor's *personal* history, and I made a promise at her grave that I wouldn't write any of that sort of thing. We Norvelters *love* her, and she *loved* us back and that is what counts. Besides, her obituary is my love letter to her and I don't want to add in any of Franklin's dirt."

"I know Mom would agree with you," I said. "But I was thinking that if President Roosevelt was so smart, how come he didn't build his Little White House in Saint Augustine and soak his damaged legs in the waters of the fountain of youth?"

She just shrugged. "I guess some men just love to be served," she speculated. "Now let's make some good time. I'm ready to see my sister."

She grew silent after that. Just like back in Norvelt, she always wore herself out telling a passionate story. It wasn't long before her breathing deepened and her head tilted over against the window and she began to snore.

Her sleeping was like a break for me. Instead of thinking of what I needed to do for her, I began to think about home. School would have started back up and I would be hanging around with Bunny again. I didn't believe that she was going to have an operation and get dead-person parts to make her taller. In fact, I think she was happy the way she was, and that was one of the big reasons why I liked her. She didn't seem to have a Dr. Jekyll and Mr. Hyde slugging it out inside her. Maybe that was because she was made up of a little of both of them and she had figured out a way to make them get along. She didn't have to choose between a totally good self and a totally bad self. She was just a happy self and said what was on her mind and went along her merry way. And that was the biggest reason why I missed her. When I was with her I didn't have to be the good me or the bad me. We were just our true selves, which was what allowed us to come together and be friends.

Just when I was having that happy thought I drove up an incline and from the top I got a long view of what was ahead of us. "Uh-oh," I announced. "More trouble in paradise."

Miss Volker woke up with a start and took a long look down the straight and narrow highway. "Spizz," she hissed. "Just the white whale I'm looking for! Now hit the gas and we'll track him down from behind."

"I thought you said you cared about people," I

228

reminded her, as the friendly thoughts of Bunny lingered in my mind.

"This is no time for a mutiny, sailor," she growled. "Now, follow orders!"

"Aye-aye, captain!" I replied.

"At a time like this," she lamented, "I wish I had a few cannon on board so we could blow that little Amphicar out of the water."

Spizz must not have seen us right away, and by the time he spotted us in his rearview mirror we were quickly gaining on him.

"Pull up side by side," she ordered. "So I can throw the harpoon right through the white whale and pierce his black heart."

"You know, I don't think you should try to kill him," I said, easing off the gas.

"Just do as I say," she demanded, and slammed her foot onto mine and floored the gas pedal. "He deserves hell on earth and I'm just the hell on wheels to give it to him."

"But isn't it like your 'tick-tock cycle of life' thing?" I hollered as the wind whipped through the car. "Like, aren't you questioning why you want to kill him, and doesn't that make you think you shouldn't?"

"No. It only makes me think I should stop his clock," she yelled back, and reached with her long, lanky arm to grab her harpoon and hold it out the window.

To get her into proper throwing position, she wanted me to swerve onto the wrong side of the road and drive up next to him. I ignored her and moved right, onto the dirt breakdown lane. Spizz was going as fast as he could and was all hunched over his steering wheel, as if leaning forward would make him go faster. It was pretty funny. I was leaning forward too, but I couldn't quite catch him and he couldn't quite pull away from me.

We rounded a curve and I could see where my dirt lane was narrowing down toward the concrete pillar of a bridge that took the highway over a river. I slowed and pulled back onto the road.

"Closer!" Miss Volker shouted. "I don't want him to escape by driving down the embankment and into the water before we plant our flag on him!"

"Then throw it now!" I shouted as I inched the VW right behind the Amphicar's fenders.

Miss Volker reared back and let it fly. It was a perfect shot. The harpoon went straight and true, and the sharp, hooked blade pierced the Amphicar on the right tail fin. I steadied my course and as the rope spooled out, the harpoon held.

"He's running for his life now," she hollered, just as all the rope we had stretched into a rigid line between us. If Miss Volker were a tightrope walker, she could have opened the car door and tiptoed across the line and grabbed Spizz from behind.

"Mind the rudder," she ordered me, "and stay right on his flukes."

Spizz looked over his shoulder and smiled. I smiled back. He lifted his hand off the wheel and gave a jolly little wave.

"I'll reel you in yet," Miss Volker hollered. "And when I do you'll be boiled down to blubber oil."

Spizz began to zigzag as he drove. He steered left and I followed. He steered right and I followed, and then he did a quick left and right and the rope slackened, but only for a moment before it abruptly pulled tight with a sudden jerk and I thought the harpoon was going to pull out of his tail fin and flip back and harpoon me between the eyes. Instead, the VW's front bumper ripped off and Spizz sped away with our bumper clanging behind him end over end like an uprooted anchor.

I backed my foot off the gas.

"Dang!" she cried out. "We lost our bowsprit and my whale weapon!"

"I don't think he's gone for good," I said. "For a guy who's hiding from the law he sure seems to be around a lot."

"That's because my love is the bait he can't resist," she said proudly, straightening out her blue hair with her smoky hands. "He's heading south for warmer waters and we'll corner him in the shallows."

After pulling into a rest area to check the damage, we got under way again. It was smooth sailing for a while until I looked in the rearview mirror and could just make out the ferret detective on his motorcycle.

"Trouble off the stern," I said. "We're still being followed."

"I've got no gun. The whale ran off with my harpoon. Now there is nothing left but to give that detective a good tongue-lashing," Miss Volker said in a threatening voice. "Besides, once he knows the truth about Spizz he'll realize he's wasting his time chasing after us, when he should really be after the killer!"

But the detective didn't catch up to us. He stayed just far enough behind to remain out of harm's way. He didn't know Miss Volker had lost her harpoon, so he wasn't taking any chances that next time she'd let him have it on the chin.

"And I haven't seen Mr. Huffer," I said, glancing in my mirrors. "Maybe he's still under repair."

"He'll show up sooner or later," she ventured. "He's a hound for money. He's eager to charge Mr. Hap a fortune to box up my sister in that fancy bomb-shelter casket, and he'll be scheming to set a trap to catch Spizz so he can get the reward."

"But what can we do?" I asked weakly. "Huffer has the gun."

"I promised Eleanor at her grave that I'd catch the killer," she replied, "so you can bet I'm working on a plan."

"Would you like to share your plan with me?" I asked. "I'm smart. Maybe I could help."

"The kind of brains you have are dangerous," she shot back. "Which reminds me, I told your mother I'd sharpen you up some, so it's time for your tutoring."

I groaned. "This is like school in a car," I said. "Hand me some beef jerky. I need some brain food."

"They don't call it *jerky* for nothing," she pointed out. "Now, since we are heading for the fountain of youth, tell me who discovered it."

"Easy. Ponce de León," I replied.

"F," she said. "Nobody discovered it, because it doesn't exist except in your imagination. So tell me, why was it invented as a story?"

"Because everyone old and tired and wrinkled wants to be young again?" I guessed, and gave her a critical look.

"I'll give you a C for that. Healing-water stories have been around forever in folklore. Every culture has its own story, but nobody can ever find the healing waters in reality. When Ponce de León was in Cuba, he was menacing the natives. To get rid of him, they told him their healing-water story about a river in Bimini that made you younger when you jumped into it. So Ponce left the natives alone and sailed toward the island of Bimini but missed it and landed in Florida."

"Did you ever see the Walt Disney cartoon where Donald Duck finds the fountain of youth?" I asked.

"Dumb comments like that make old people not want to be young again," she snapped. "Anyway, Ponce had not taken a bath once in his entire voyage from Spain to Cuba, but legend has it that once he got to Florida he plunged into every pool of water, stream, and river he could find.

"He got bad diarrhea from drinking tainted water, and went a little nuts from dragging his naked butt across the grass like a dog. Then finally he came upon some local people who said there was a river that kept people young. The river was named Apalachicola, which in the native language meant They-Help-Each-Other River. So Ponce jumped in and all the natives jumped in and they started to help each other catch fish. The natives knew that helping each other is truly the *magic* that keeps people young. Eleanor Roosevelt knew that too, which is why Norvelt was built as a help-each-other town. But Ponce de León didn't want fish. He wanted youth. So he cut off a few heads and created a fountain of blood and left."

"So you can't jump in a puddle and become a kid

again," I said, summing up her story like I was concluding a research paper for class.

"Well," she said, pondering the thought, "Saint John the Baptist dunked people in water so they would be born again and cleansed of sin."

"So would they crawl out of the water wearing a diaper and drinking from a baby bottle?" I asked.

"Look at it this way," she replied. "The great French thinker Rousseau said, 'All men are born free, but everywhere they are in chains.' And this is so universally true that people want to believe that when they are in the chains of old age, or chained down by their evil sins, or chained down by corrupt governments, they can somehow return to their newborn selves and start over. So jumping into a lake and becoming young, and cleaned of sin, and having lifelong freedom is an infantile fantasy which is very appealing, but it doesn't solve any real problems."

"So there is no fountain of youth, right?"

"A-plus," she replied. "Except if you want to believe in it in your imagination."

"Well, I'm already young," I said, "so I don't have to imagine it."

"And I'm just old and desperate enough to want to believe in it," she replied with her voice rising. "I'm a dreamer, and right now my dream is to have a gallon of that water because this bucket of hot coals is just about to set me on fire." She lifted up her legs and I could see where her stockings were smoking.

I downshifted and quickly pulled over to the side of the road and removed the bucket. Well behind us, the police motorcycle pulled over too. I scooped up sand and covered the coals. By the time I made sure the fire was out and returned to the car, I found Miss Volker had fallen asleep again. Teaching me history lessons must have been an exhausting job for her.

I just kept driving as fast as possible and scanning my mirrors for the detective and whoever might want to come after us. Sometimes the motorcycle was right behind us, sometimes it wasn't.

Once in a while I got drowsy and jerked my head around to wake myself up. To keep myself alert, I played little games like keeping count of other green cars on the road. I rechecked my mirrors every so often to see if anyone was sneaking up on us, but the coast was clear and the road was smooth. There was nothing more I could do but drive and get Miss Volker where she wanted to go.

Since she was in a deep sleep I took a chance and turned on the radio. It was all static.

"That's the sound of Hitler's brain now," she said with her eyes closed.

It was annoying and I turned it off. "Did they ever find Hitler's brain?" I asked.

"The Russians probably got it," she guessed. "And they hid it inside Stalin's skull. When he died they offered it to Khrushchev and he seems to be using about half of it."

"Maybe it's up in *Sputnik*," I said, "making that *beep-beep-beep* sound."

Just then I heard the sound of a tire blow, and the steering wheel pulled to the side. I slowed down and veered off the road until I found a solid patch of rocky ground. I stopped and yanked up the parking brake.

"Flat tire," she said.

I hopped out and walked around the VW. "Front right," I called out.

"Open the hood," she replied.

I knew the tire and tools were in there. I removed the spare and jack and plastic pouch of tire tools. I had changed flats on our tractor in Norvelt so I knew what to do. I worked quickly because I was afraid the creepy detective might show up when we were a sitting duck on the side of the road. In no time I had the car jacked up and the lug nuts loosened. I removed the flat tire and fitted the good one onto the bolts. Quickly I tightened the nuts and lowered the car.

Right then I looked over my shoulder and saw the

detective far down the road. I didn't wait to put the tools away. I ran around to my side, jumped in, started the engine, and took off.

I followed the map. We had left Georgia and were hauling through north Florida. The road was flat and straight and Miss Volker dozed on and off.

We were just outside of Saint Augustine when Miss Volker sat up and rubbed the sleep from her eyes.

"Welcome to the Sunshine State," I said when she stretched her arms and yawned. "We are almost at your swimming hole."

"I need to warm up my hands before swimming," she said. "They cooled down again. Pull into a restaurant."

"It's not good to eat before you swim," I reminded her.

"Who said anything about eating?" she replied.

"I don't think that nap helped you," I suggested. "The farther south we go, the grumpier you get."

"There's no turning back now," she said. "Just wait until I get to Miami. By then my mood will be criminal!"

So I turned into the entrance of the first restaurant I came to. It was a soup and salad joint.

We walked in and took a seat at a table. Our waiter gave us menus, and before he walked off Miss Volker quickly glanced at hers and said, "May I have two bowls of split pea soup?"

"Miss Volker," I whispered. "I don't like split pea soup."

"I didn't order any for you," she said crossly. "Get your own food."

She turned back to the waiter while I read the menu.

"And make that soup extra hot," she instructed.

"Spicy hot?" he asked, as he wrote a note on the order pad.

"Not *spicy*!" she hollered. "I said *hot*! Like *boiling hot*!"

"Okay, ma'am," he replied. "Coming right up."

I ordered a grilled cheese sandwich off the kids' menu, with extra pickles.

The moment the waiter left I leaned forward. "Miss Volker, how can anyone like that much split pea soup?" I asked. "It's disgusting."

"It's good for what ails me," she replied. "You'll see. A couple bowls of split pea soup and I can backstroke around that pool at the fountain of youth."

In a moment our meals arrived. "Is the soup hot enough for you?" the waiter asked with a wise-guy smile on his face.

The soup looked like green lava. Steaming bubbles were rising up and popping on the surface. If there was a fly in her soup, it was boiled alive.

She smiled up at the waiter. "Just right," she said in a little old-granny voice. "Not too hot and not too cold."

"Enjoy," he said, and as he dashed back to the kitchen

she held her hands over the bowls. The steam beaded up on her palms, and then after a quick fingertip test, like sticking her toe into a scalding-hot tub of water, she gently lowered her hands into the soup until the thick green bog of liquid covered them.

"Help me," she said with her teeth clenched and her neck muscles all flexed and red. "Cover my hands with your napkins so people don't stare."

She didn't have to tell me twice. I unfolded the cloth napkins and tented them over her hands.

"The smell of this vile soup makes me want to sneeze," she said. "Quick, a handkerchief."

I pulled mine out of my jacket and held it under her nose. She sneezed and I wiped her nose and shoved it into my back pocket, which suddenly reminded me of something.

"I forgot to tell you," I whispered excitedly, "what Mr. Huffer told me on the train when he was playing like a detective. He said that if I had any information on how to catch you and Spizz that I should hang a hand-kerchief out of my back pocket at the funeral parlor."

"Why are you telling me this when I feel like I'm being boiled in oil?" she asked, with her jaw jutting in and out like a spastic desk drawer.

"I thought it might be important," I replied.

"This torture should be against the Geneva Convention," she hissed, and began to scuttle her shoes back and forth across the wooden floor.

"Well, is what I said important?" I asked.

"Press your shoes down on my shoes and anchor them to the floor," she said. "It's important that I don't blast off like a bottle rocket."

I pressed down on her shoes and she bucked back and forth in her chair. Soon, beneath the napkins, I could see the shape of her fingers moving around as they came to life like frozen snakes warming up under the sun. Before long she was making a fist with each hand.

"This feels better," she said, smiling with relief. "Holding them over the bucket fire was like barbecuing pig's feet—it was a dry heat. But this soup is as thick and creamy as any wax I've used."

Just then the waiter returned. "How is the soup?" he asked.

"De-licious," she replied, and lifted her bright red hands out of the bowls. "But I suggest you try it with a couple of these old ham bones—they really give it a special flavor." She grinned up at him.

He looked at me for an explanation.

"Which way is the men's room?" I asked.

He pointed out the back door. I went outside and there was only a little shack. It smelled pretty rank inside. When I came out I took a walk because I needed some fresh air, and it felt good to stretch my legs after the long drive.

And then I saw the police motorcycle with the side-car parked behind the trash cans. I turned and ran to the rear door of the restaurant, but it was too late. He must have been spying on us, and the moment I left he had slipped in behind my back. The ferret detective was sitting in my seat and he was listening eagerly to Miss Volker. Then he was saying something to her and I could see that he had his hand jammed deeply into his jacket pocket and the fabric on the outside was pointy, like he was holding onto a pistol. I didn't think he would do anything to her while they were inside the restaurant, so I returned to his motorcycle. There was a small zipped case in the sidecar and I unzipped it. His notebook was in there and under it was his pistol, only it was broken. The barrel was slightly bent to the side where it had dropped out of his hand and gone bouncing end over end down the road. Now, either he had another pistol or, like a lousy bank robber, he was using his pointer finger as a fake gun.

I turned around and went back inside the restaurant, but he was gone. I ran over to the table. "Where'd the detective go?" I asked.

"Miami," she said. "He's after the killer and the reward money."

"Did you tell him anything else?"

"I told him to drop dead," she said.

"Did you see the fake gun in his pocket?"

"Why bother looking?" she replied. "He's not going to shoot me in a soup and salad joint."

The waiter came by and handed me the bill. I reached into my back pocket and pulled out my wallet. I plucked out a few dollars and set them on the table.

"This should cover it," I said. "With a tip."

"I got a tip for you," he said. "Hit the road. Get on out of here before we serve her up on a plate."

When we went outside Miss Volker handed me a dinner knife she had taken from the table. "Open the other can of paint," she said. "It's time for a new look."

"Right," I said. I opened the can and poured some on the hood and stroked it back and forth with the stiff green brush. I kept pouring and painting and when I was finished it looked like we were driving a rotten Florida orange that was leaking orange juice and frog guts.

I tossed the bucket and brush in the trash and got Miss Volker in the car. "Keep your hands on the hot dashboard," I said, and we followed the signs that read "This Way to the Fountain of Youth."

At the first stoplight she said, "Look at my face."

I did.

"Now, watch my face as I make a frown." Slowly

243

her forehead furrowed into deep creases, her eyes became pouty slits, and her mouth and all the skin around it turned down as if gravity had reached up and tugged on her chin.

"Now," she said, still looking gloomy, "I'm going to smile on the count of three, but watch how long it takes my skin to change from a downward frown to an upward smile. One, two, three," she counted.

The corners of her mouth went up but nothing else happened right away. Then slowly, like watching a photo develop, her expression began to switch over. Her forehead lines softened and smoothed out. Her eyes sparkled. Her chin pulled up tightly, as if lifted by the leather chinstrap on a hat.

"There," she said despondently. "Look how long it took—about a minute or more to go from one expression to the next."

The light had turned green and the car behind me beeped its horn. I shifted into gear and took off.

"When you get old," she said, "you have to plan your expressions in advance or people think you are happy when you are sad and sad when you are happy. It stinks getting old. That fountain of youth better work, even though I know better. But ever since I was a kid I wanted to come here. If nothing else it will be fun, and I can use some fun."

"Fun keeps you young," I said. "Look at me."

"You look like a bloody mess," she said.

When we arrived at the Genuine Ponce de León Fountain of Youth spa we went inside and I bought one ticket.

"I'm just her lifeguard," I said to the attendant.

She shrugged and continued to file her nails.

"I need some money," Miss Volker said. "I have to buy a bathing costume."

I gave her just about all the money I had left. In a few minutes, she came out of the spa's store and made her way into the ladies' changing room with her purchase.

When she returned I looked at her without really trying to see her because I don't think I had ever seen a lady as old as Miss Volker in a two-piece bathing suit.

I had to blur my eyes at first because she sort of looked like a wrinkly plucked chicken with brightly colored elastic fabric triangles across her top and another down lower. Honestly, I didn't want to make eye contact with any part of her below her neck, and even then I was uncomfortable because if she was a chicken, the neck is where the cleaver would come down. That thought made me feel a little more sympathetic toward how she looked.

I held out my hand. "May I?" I asked, and extended

my hand as she carefully clutched it with her still-bendable fingers. We walked through an open doorway and out to a patio area encircled by tropical plants. The pool was surrounded by the patio and palm and banana trees. There was a little fountain feature in the middle of the pool that put out a musical tinkling of water.

Next to the steps that led into the water was a sign that read:

SUBMERGE YOURSELF COMPLETELY
UNDER WATER AND HOLD YOUR BREATH.
FOR EACH SECOND YOU HOLD YOUR
BREATH A YEAR WILL BE
SUBTRACTED OFF YOUR AGE.

"Okay," I said, feeling a bit skeptical after reading the sign.

She walked slowly down the steps and stood in the water up to her chin.

"On the count of three, take a deep breath and dunk your head under."

"If it works," she warned me, "you might want to avert your eyes because I weighed a lot more when I was younger and this bathing suit might snap off if I expand. In fact, you better duck too, because if this suit hits you at the speed of light, it'll knock you unconscious."

"I *promise* I'll look away," I said. "Don't worry about that."

She took a deep breath. I knew it wasn't going to work. I'm sure she did too. It was never like her to believe in something this superstitious and romantic, like a frog turned into a prince when kissed by a princess.

"One . . . two . . . three," I counted out, and she went under like a stone. "One Mississippi," I counted, "two Mississippi." I was on a forty Mississippi count when she came up for air like a whale breaking the surface. Her face was bright red and she was coughing a bit, but not bad enough that I had to resuscitate her.

"You look forty years younger," I remarked.

"And you are a liar," she sputtered. "But I feel good. The water is warm, amniotically warm. I feel like I'm my old self again."

"*Which* old self?" I asked. "Are you the nice old lady who loves Eleanor Roosevelt or the whale-obsessed Mrs. Captain Ahab? Or are you Dr. Jekyll or Mr. Hyde? Or Thomas Hughes building a failed utopia?"

"We'll have to wait and see," she said. "A true fountain of youth doesn't take years off your life—it just dissolves all the tortures of your conscience and takes you back to a golden age of youthful purity." She looked up at me and pointed toward my heart.

"Me?" I asked. "Youthful purity?"

"Yes," she replied. "Every child has a pure heart that pumps a fountain of youth through his veins."

"I don't know what you are talking about," I said, puzzled, "because I think awful stuff all the time."

"Like what?" she asked.

"Like I thought *you* had killed all those old ladies," I admitted. "It is not pure of heart to think you are a *murderer*!"

"Well," she said wistfully, "honesty is also a sign of being pure of heart."

"Then you are pure of heart," I quickly pointed out, "because you are *extra* honest!"

She waved that statement away with the back of her hand. "Now help me out of here," she demanded. "The water is giving me even more wrinkles."

I extended my hand and steadied her up the pool steps. She went to change and I found a pay phone and called home. This operator wasn't as patient as the last one. I placed a collect call to Mom, and when she said Mrs. Gantos wasn't home the operator began to hang up.

But before the final click I did hear Mom shout out, "He's in Florida!"

Dad's here, I thought, and he's looking for work, and probably looking for me. After I drop Miss Volker off it would be great to fly back to Norvelt in his plane.

I went back to the car and Miss Volker was waiting for me. Her hair was piled up on her head like the pelt of a wet poodle.

"Miss Volker," I said as I pulled out onto the road. "I think this part of the trip has been the best so far."

"Yeah," she said, and sighed deeply. "Stress-free for the moment."

"The next is not so good, is it?" I asked.

"Miami will be trouble *without* paradise. It will be the worst," she said. "Worse than the sorrow at Hyde Park. Worse than the humiliation at Rugby. Even worse than you falling into a septic tank," she said with humor, and elbowed me in the ribs.

"But could anything be worse than your Mrs. Captain Ahab imitation?" I asked.

"Your crappy comic book reading is far worse," she replied with contempt.

"Well, nothing can be worse than your snoring," I shot right back.

"Ha. Your paint job on this car is the worst!"

"Your lousy eating habits are pathetic," I said, and stuck out my tongue.

"And you need a bath," she said, pinching her nose. "You smell the worst."

"Thanks for reminding me," I said. "But there is nothing worse than old-lady smell."

"When's the last time you changed your underwear?" she asked, and rolled down her window for some fresh air.

"Probably the last time you changed yours," I replied.

"Well," she said smugly. "I washed mine in the fountain of youth."

"Well, it didn't make it young and fresh again," I replied, and rolled my window down.

This last jab seemed to hurt. She went quiet, and I felt bad for not realizing that a little part of her wanted the fountain of youth to be real.

"When you get old," she said after a while, "you smell like you are slowly dying, and there is no cure for that."

"Sure there is," I said. "Hang out with me all day. You'll still be old on the outside, but on the inside you'll be youthfully immature."

"No time for immaturity," she said, and pulled herself up ramrod straight in her seat. "Let's get one good night of sleep and we'll face the enemy in the morning."

We pulled in to the Ponce de León Motor Inn.

13

I slept oddly at the motel and woke up early in the morning feeling very different from myself. It's like when I fall asleep while reading and the story jumps tracks and rolls along like a ghost train. In my sleep, I find myself left behind like some character in the story who has been dropped off at the wrong station. Somehow I realize I have to find my way back into the correct book. I leave the station and drift down an unknown street, and instead of finding my book I open the front cover of a random house I have never been to before.

When I step inside, there are hundreds of rooms and each wall is a printed page of the book that left me behind. I read for a long time and finally I enter a room and read a wall and catch up to the page where I left off when I fell asleep. I learn what became of all the characters, and all their intentions, and if they had a good or bad ending.

By the time I finish reading my way through the rooms of the story and close the back cover, I stroll away as if I have become another person. It's odd to wake up feeling different from when you went to sleep, but I like how the old me and the new me become another me.

Now, after traveling with Miss Volker, I felt like a character trying to catch up with himself. Maybe the same thing had happened to Miss Volker. Only she seemed to know a lot more about who she was and what was going on, and it was as if she and I were in the same book, only she was well ahead of me in knowing the story. I always read books very slowly and she was a fast reader. Maybe she knew she was getting close to the last page and had just about figured out the ending, while I was lagging behind and still hadn't put it all together. Either way, the somber mood of the morning seemed to be very different from the mood of the night before.

When we pulled out of the motel parking lot she looked preoccupied. I stayed quiet and waited to hear what was on her mind.

"In *Moby-Dick*," she started, "there comes a time when Captain Ahab, after all his searching, thinks that maybe he won't find the white whale and his trip will be for naught."

"I don't think that part was in the Classics Illustrated version," I said, trying to recall.

"Well, read the real book someday," she advised. "I've been in Norvelt since 1934 and now I too am wondering if I'll ever find my prey—and if I do find him, will I be driven to kill him as Captain Ahab was, or will I kiss him on his big fishy lips?"

"Does this mean you are giving up on catching Spizz?" I asked.

"No, I'm not giving up," she said. "I'm not dead yet but I'm just not as angry at him. For some reverse reason, chasing him has made me like him a bit more."

"Well, I can help you replenish your anger," I said, trying to do her a favor. "On the train, Spizz told me that the two of you worked together to kill the old ladies so you would be free to marry him."

"That's a lie," she snapped back. "He is a lie factory. He's a Ponzi scheme of lies—a person tells him the truth and in return he gives them two lies."

"What's a Ponzi?" I asked. I thought a question might cheer her up.

"*He* was a cheater," she said. "A Boston crook in 1920. He promised people huge returns on their investments with him. In the beginning he did pay people big returns, but that was just a trick to lure in even bigger investors. In the end Ponzi tried to run off with everyone's money, but he was caught and jailed. Now the name Ponzi is forever linked with being a cheater."

"And the name Spizz?" I asked. "What will that be forever linked to?"

She thought about it. "I guess it will forever be linked to me being a love cheater. I love that he loves me, but I don't love him. I enjoy keeping him around but I never let him get close to me. He tortures me a little and I torture him back twice the amount, and that is not the Norvelt way. If I was a good person, I would either love him or leave him. I'd make a decision and stick with it."

"But you're stuck in the middle?" I said, gathering up her thoughts.

"Yep," she said. "Captain Ahab had mixed feelings for the white whale. He loved him, but he feared him too. He was tortured by his mixed feelings. Finally he had to make a decision, so he decided to kill the whale to put an end to the feelings fighting within himself. Either the whale or Ahab dies—they can't live together in the same book."

"Can't you try to live with both feelings?" I asked, knowing that Ahab was the one who died, dragged under the sea by the rope of his own harpoon after he'd speared his whale.

"I don't think so," she said. "My feelings for Spizz are going to fight to the death inside me," she added. "There is no separating them, and just like Jekyll and Hyde, one of them has to go. It's the good, or the evil. They can't live together."

"So what's next?"

"All I know is that before the world ends I want my kiss," she said. "I want my little bit of love."

"With a killer?" I asked.

"No," she said. "I can't kiss a filthy killer."

"Then what are you getting at?" I asked.

"There are just some days," she said, "that are lived out like the last page of a book, and I think today is one of those days."

"What happens tomorrow?" I asked.

"You start a new book," she replied. "Now pull over," she said. "I have to make a phone call."

I did. There was a row of phones, and I went to one end and she went to the other. I called Mom.

"I accept the charges," Mom quickly replied to the operator, once I asked for her. "I'll make this fast," she said. "Your father has been in touch with Mr. Hap and will meet you at some point in Miami."

"What will happen to Miss Volker?" I asked.

"Mr. Hap will take care of her," she said. "He'll drive back up here with her once her sister's body is shipped to Norvelt for burial."

"Okay," I said. "Anything else?"

"How's your rash?" she asked. "Are you using that special cream?"

"I gotta run," I said. "Miss Volker's waiting for me."

After I hung up, I started the car while Miss Volker finished her call. When she did, she was in a big hurry.

"Okay," she said, as she got back into the car and I pulled out into traffic. "This is what we do. Drive to Miami to the Vizcaya Funeral Parlor. Huffer is arriving today to drop off the casket. Hap has had my sister's body embalmed, and once she is in the casket we'll have a porthole viewing this afternoon and a little service, and her body will be shipped home with Mr. Huffer as escort."

"Okay," I said. "I washed my face but my clothes look pretty awful."

"Don't worry. You'll be at a funeral parlor," she pointed out. "Nobody looks worse than dead people."

"Do I need to be on the lookout for the detective or Spizz? Or anyone?" I asked, checking my mirrors.

"No," she said. "That's all behind us. Now we just take care of my sister."

I hit the gas and we got on the Florida turnpike. Our little VW held together and we made it to Miami by midafternoon.

I called the funeral home from a gas station to get

directions. It was next to a large cemetery by the high-way. When we pulled into the parking lot, Miss Volker glanced at herself in the rearview mirror.

"Well," she said, and poked at her matted hair. The Fountain of Youth had washed all the blue out of it and now the humidity had curled it into a knotted mass of gray Spanish moss. "My hair and this weather are at war with each other. Everybody in a funeral parlor has a role to play and I guess I better get all dolled up to play mine. I'm going inside to the ladies' room and will see you at the viewing."

"Okay," I said. "I'd try to clean up my shirt but it's hopeless for me."

"No," she said, and opened her door. "You are clue-less, not hopeless. There is a difference."

I let her walk into the funeral parlor on her own because I wasn't as clueless as she thought. I gave her a minute to get to the bathroom and then I dashed in-side. There was a sign pointing to a VIEWING AND SER-VICE FOR MRS. VALDENE HAP.

I marched down the hall and entered the correct room. Mr. Hap was sitting in a wingback chair with his hands covering his face. He was quietly sobbing, so I left him alone. I was waiting for someone else.

In a minute, Mr. Huffer walked into the room with his carrying case.

"Hello, Mr. Huffer," I quietly said.

He gave me a distrustful look. "The last time I saw you I believe you were digging a grave. Did you ever put someone in it?"

"Nope," I replied.

"Too bad," he said. "That was a waste of good digging."

"So how do you like Florida?" I asked, trying to make small talk.

"I like it a lot," he replied. "There's money to be made down here. What do you think is Florida's biggest export crop?"

"Oranges?"

"Nope."

"Alligators?"

"Nope. Give up?"

"Yep."

"Caskets," he said. "Full caskets. There are so many retired people in Florida and they are dropping like flies. Every train and plane out of here is full of dead people. Once I make some money, I'll open a funeral parlor down here and clean up."

When he said *money* I dropped my pen behind my back and bent over to pick it up. I took my time and shook my rear around until he saw the handkerchief waving in my pocket.

"Jack," he said quietly, and glanced back at Mr. Hap. "Come over here. Why is that handkerchief in your pocket?"

"You know why," I whispered, and gave him a knowing look.

He smiled.

"What else do you have for me?" he asked.

"Miss Volker planned all the murders and Spizz did all the dirty work," I whispered. "I overheard them talking and wrote it all down." I gave him a folded piece of paper.

"Good job," he replied, but when he opened it he looked puzzled.

"It's in Esperanto," I explained. "Code. Just in case Spizz or Miss Volker caught me ratting them out. I signed it on the bottom."

He nodded as he folded up the note and slipped it into his jacket pocket. "I'll get the jump on Spizz at the viewing," he said, "before we ship the casket up north."

"Now can you pay me my money?" I asked, sticking out my hand. "Half the reward."

"I won't have the money until Spizz is out of the way," he said, again glancing back at Mr. Hap. "He's the one who confessed, so no problem collecting the reward."

"But I want my money now," I insisted. "I'm only doing this to help out my family."

"Keep your voice down," he said. "Believe me, I want the money even more than you do. Just be patient and let me polish off this funeral job. The other funeral director didn't know what Valdene looked like so I said I'd make up her face for the viewing."

I followed Mr. Huffer to the front of the room, where two attendants had rolled in the bombproof porthole casket. It was sitting on a metal table with wheels on the bottom so it could be rolled to the back of Huffer's hearse. Mr. Hap was in a black suit, and was now snuffling into a hankie.

Mr. Huffer glanced at him and shook his head contemptuously. "*Crybaby*," he mouthed to me. "Now let me touch up her face to make sure she looks as cantankerous as her twin sister."

The casket was covered with a red velvet cloth. Mr. Huffer pulled it off and neatly folded it into a square and set it aside. The first thing he noticed was the open vent on the end of the casket. "That's a mistake," he remarked, and slid it shut. "You only keep it open if you are using it as a bomb shelter." Then he leaned over the glass porthole on the casket and frowned. "I told that guy not to make up her face," he said unpleasantly. "Whoever did her face is a klutz. Look at the lipstick! I bet your Miss Volker with her lousy hands botched this up. A kindergartner could do a better job. And look at that witchy hair!"

I moved in to get a closer look. It *was* awful. The lipstick was smeared around her mouth like the Joker from *Batman* and her hair stood out like she had been hit by lightning.

"I'll touch it up," he said, clearly annoyed. "But even a real artist like me can do only so much to make the dead look alive."

With that, Mr. Hap let out a high-pitched wail behind his handkerchief. "She was so beautiful," he cried as the words staggered out of his quivering mouth.

Mr. Huffer gave him a pathetic look. "I'm not a miracle worker," he said with a note of cruelty in his voice. "She *is* old."

Mr. Hap turned and buried his face in a little cherub-shaped pillow as he wept.

Mr. Huffer rolled his eyes as he set his makeup case on the floor and snapped it open. Rows of small trays folded out like stair steps, and each tray was filled with some item to help the dead look slightly less dead. I had seen that case before when Bunny made me up to look like Mr. Spizz.

Mr. Huffer reached into the case and pulled out an open sleeve of Girl Scout cookies. "Want a Thin Mint?" he asked. "They are a breath of fresh air in this heat."

Not on your life, I thought. "No thanks," I replied.

He ate one, then removed a compact and brush, a tube of lipstick, and a packet of cotton wipes. He put them in his pocket and with great effort he lifted the top of the steel casket. "Extra heavy," he grunted once he had it open.

"Atomic-bomb proof," I said with admiration.

He leaned over Mrs. Hap's face and with a cotton swab touched her lips.

At that instant she let out a mummified groan.

"Oh cheeze!" I yelped, and hopped back.

Mr. Huffer looked at me with annoyance. "It's just escaping gas," he snapped. "Show some guts for a change. And if your sissy nose starts bleeding, take it outside."

The moment he bent forward to continue his cosmetic work on Mrs. Hap her arms suddenly reached up and her hands tried to clutch the lapels on his jacket. "Arghhhh!" she growled.

Mr. Huffer's eyes bugged out as he slapped hysterically at her hands. She grabbed his tie, but his fear was his strength and he wriggled out of her grip and leaped back in horror.

"Was that gas?" I asked.

"Shut up!" he snapped, then turned back to the body. "Who are you?" he demanded.

"Your nightmare," she cried out.

"Cheeze!" I yelped again, and jigged up and down like a monkey-boy. "She's alive!"

"Did you say *alive*?" Mr. Hap shouted out from behind his handkerchief.

"You bet I'm alive," she spit back. "I'm not poor dead Valdene. I'm Miss Volker, who you've been bothering for days, and I know you killed those old ladies and you aren't going to kill me too."

Mr. Huffer stiffened and turned pale, but from working on the dead for so long he quickly regained his composure. He pulled the pistol from his coat pocket and pointed it at her. "Say your prayers. I told you this casket is wide. We'll have a twin killing and I'll bury you with your sister and then take care of that moron, Spizz."

"What about me?" I asked. "What will you do to me?"

"I think a packing crate to China without a return address will do for you," he said as if he had been planning it that way from the beginning.

"And me?" blubbered Mr. Hap from behind his pillow. "What will you do with me?"

"Alligators eat crybabies for breakfast out in the Everglades," Mr. Huffer replied. "Someday I might be wearing you as a belt or a pair of shoes."

At that moment Miss Volker leaned forward and

reached toward him with her stiff hands. "Go ahead and shoot," she said. "I dare you."

"Cheeze-us-crust!" I squealed. "Don't *dare* him!"

"Shut up!" he said to me without taking his eyes off of her.

"Right here," she begged him, and tapped herself on her chest. "Just like in Rugby."

"You're going to go from *playing* dead to being dead," he said. "I've had it with you." He aimed for her heart and pulled the trigger. *Click*. He pulled it again and the cylinder on the pistol rotated. *Click*. He kept pulling the trigger. She reached forward with her other hand and slowly unfolded her nimble fingers. There were five bullets.

"Now give me the gun," she said.

"Your hands," he remarked.

"I soaked them in the fountain of youth," she replied smartly. "It works."

I was spellbound by her hands. Maybe the fountain of youth was for real.

"Mr. Huffer," Mr. Hap said with authority, standing up and removing the handkerchief from across his face. "You are under arrest for murder." He held out a badge and I saw that he was not Mr. Hap at all. He was the ferret-faced private detective from the train, and he snatched the gun from Huffer's hand. He reached for the bullets and nervously inserted them into the cylinder.

"You can't arrest me," Huffer said. "I've done nothing wrong. I was trying to protect myself from a deranged lunatic."

"Rubbish," said Miss Volker in the casket.

Suddenly the real Mr. Hap pulled aside the velvet curtain that hung behind the casket. Another Miss Volker was wearing the same dress and had the same sloppy makeup. I looked at the body in the casket that was alive but supposed to be dead, and back at the one who was supposed to be dead but was alive—and she winked at me.

Mr. Huffer stepped back toward the door and the detective swiftly blocked his exit and aimed the gun at his back.

The not-dead-yet Miss Volker continued to lower the boom on Mr. Huffer. "You murdered all those old ladies. We knew there was something fishy about you when you started selling their homes. And then the detective here"—she nodded toward him—"filled us in on the details. The police have been tracking down the phony company where the fake old-lady insurance policies came from. And now they have evidence that you are behind them. Those policies wouldn't pay out benefits in the case of murder, so as the ladies got older you had to kill them to keep from going broke."

"Nonsense," Huffer sputtered. "All lies."

"And," she continued, "since Spizz stupidly confessed, you figured all you had to do was kill or capture him and you could collect the reward on top of everything else!"

"I'm confused," I said.

The standing Miss Volker turned toward me. "I faked my sister's death to help me catch the killer," she said. "You knew I thought it was Spizz at first, so I invited Huffer down to make the death look real. I didn't want Spizz to get suspicious of the plan."

"How did you know he would come?" I asked.

"History quiz time," the real Miss Volker suddenly said to me.

"At a time like this?" I moaned. "Really?"

"There is never a time when being stupid is good," she said. "So answer me this: Who was the ex-president who represented Eleanor Roosevelt at her wedding to Franklin Roosevelt?"

"Easy-peasy," I answered. "Teddy Roosevelt."

"Exactly," she replied. "And like someone said of Teddy Roosevelt, 'He has to be the bride at every wedding and the corpse at every funeral.' And Huffer is the same way."

"I'm still confused," I said.

"I'm the sister with the good hands," said the Miss Volker in the casket, as she cracked her knuckles like a tough guy before climbing out. Mr. Hap stepped around the casket to give her a hand.

My Miss Volker smiled and held up her claws. "And I'm the bad-hands twin," she said.

The detective poked Mr. Huffer in the back with the pistol. "How about you tell us how you poisoned them?" he suggested.

"I did nothing of the sort," Mr. Huffer said indignantly.

"Then why don't you climb into the casket and think about it," the detective said, and gave him another good jab in the back with the pistol. "I'm driving you back to Norvelt, where the police are waiting for you."

"What?" Mr. Huffer exclaimed.

"You heard him," said my Miss Volker. "You said it was big enough for more than one, so it should be spacious enough for you."

Huffer looked at all of us as if we were mad.

"I'll tell you what," said the detective. "You better climb inside or I'll give the gun to Miss Volker and this time she'll have bullets."

I helpfully pulled a chair over to the table and casket. Huffer put his foot on the seat, then climbed up and stepped one foot into the casket, and then the other. Slowly he lowered himself until he was in the proper dead-man position. "I might just as well die," he groaned.

"You better give me your car keys," ordered the detective. "I can't strap this casket onto my side car."

Mr. Huffer dutifully fished them out of his jacket pocket.

Mr. Hap lowered the metal lid and secured the clasp on the outside. I went to the end of the casket and opened the vent so Mr. Huffer could breathe.

"What do we do now?" Miss Volker asked.

"Let's roll him to the hearse," said the detective, "and I'll drive him home in a casket even Houdini couldn't escape."

He handed Miss Volker her pistol, and we all got behind the wheeled table and rolled Mr. Huffer out of the viewing room and down the hall and through the front door. We were in the parking lot when I heard the whine of an airplane overhead. I looked up just as Dad's J-3 swooped down and wiggled its wings. If he saw the twin Miss Volkers he must have wondered who we had in the casket. Maybe he thought they were triplets. As we continued to load Mr. Huffer into the back of the hearse Dad circled around and eventually landed in an unused portion at the back of the cemetery beside the funeral parlor.

"The police will need you all to testify against Mr. Huffer," the detective informed us. "I'll be in touch."

"We'll do everything you need us to do," replied a smiling Mrs. Hap. Her lipstick had seeped out into the grid of lines around her mouth so that her face looked like a street map.

The detective tugged on the heavy door of the hearse and then stepped inside and slammed it. When he settled down in his seat he looked pretty small, and I wondered if he could reach the pedals and see out the windshield at the same time. Mr. Huffer might appreciate that bombproof coffin more than he does now, I thought, just in case they drive off a cliff.

As the detective drove away with Mr. Huffer we all waved, but when I lowered my hand my heart lowered too. What would become of Bunny? I wanted to talk to her. I could just imagine if I called her collect the operator would ask her, "Do you accept the charges?" And Bunny would shout back, "My dad is innocent of all charges!" No matter what, she would stick up for him. And as a friend, no matter what, I would make sure to stick up for her.

Suddenly Dad came running over.

"Hey," he said anxiously. "I'm double-parked next to an open grave, so we better get going."

"Going where?" I asked.

"To meet Spizz," said Miss Volker, with an enigmatic smile on her face.

"Are you going to try to get your harpoon back?" I asked.

"I'll tell you everything in the plane," she said.

Miss Volker gave her sister a hug and a kiss, and Dad encouraged them to hurry up, then turned and ran ahead of us. I glanced over at the VW. I loved that car. Miss Volker had kissed a picture of Mrs. Roosevelt goodbye, so I ran over and gave that good German car a great big kiss right on the hood. "I'll be back," I whispered. "Wait for me."

I pulled the keys out of my pocket and gave them to Mr. Hap as I shook his hand. Valdene's lips were a little scary, so I just gave her a hug.

"We'll see you soon," she said, with a little secret in her voice.

Then Miss Volker and I held hands and marched off as quickly as we could. Once we were seated in the plane Dad opened up the throttle. The engine roared and we scooted across a bumpy, empty patch at the back of the cemetery. Just before a row of gravestones the wheels lifted off the ground and the tail end of the J-3 swooped back and forth like a sailboat on the water. Every puff of wind knocked us from starboard to port as we climbed higher and circled around.

Miss Volker leaned forward from the backseat and looked out the side window at the rows of gravestones. "That's a patchwork quilt of history down there," she remarked.

"Kind of an underground library," I suggested.

"That's a good way to look at it," she agreed, "though I'd rather be buried in a book than in a casket."

"It won't take long before we land in the Glades," Dad said above the engine noise. "So you two better get to saying your goodbyes."

Miss Volker took my hand and squeezed it between hers. "You are the best friend an old lady ever had," she said with tears in her eyes. "When I was a hothead you told me to be patient. I could have killed Spizz a dozen times, but you told me not to jump to conclusions."

"Did Spizz know about this plan to catch the killer?" I asked.

"Of course not," Miss Volker replied. "Because in the beginning I thought he was the killer. Later on, I thought differently. Believe me, when I held the pistol against Huffer's chest that night in Rugby I wasn't quite sure he was the murderer either. That's why I pulled the bullets out just in case my fingers did work and I plugged him."

Something else occurred to me. "What if Huffer had bought more bullets after Rugby?"

"Well, there was that possibility, but it was a chance I had to take," she said. "I gave my word to Mrs. Roosevelt at her gravesite that I'd catch the killer and I did."

"When were you totally sure?" I asked.

"The little detective told me at the restaurant that it was Huffer who secretly owned the predatory life insurance company. And worse," she added, "it was his wife who sold the policies to the old ladies."

"That is just what Spizz said! I guess I was wrong about him," I confessed.

"We both were," she admitted. "Then you really pulled a good one on Huffer with that handkerchief in your pocket bit. He jumped for joy over that Esperanto confession he thought would get him the reward on Spizz."

"Little did he know the note was just a few lines from Lincoln's Gettysburg Address—in pig Latin," I revealed slyly.

"*A-plus* for that," she stressed. "He's somebody who wouldn't recognize history even when it's right in front of him."

"You really had me believing you were going to kill Spizz," I said.

"I told you that I love him as much as I want to kill him," she declared. "I'm really Jekyll and Hyde. I'm the one who told Spizz to sneak back to Norvelt and we'd run off together, since I promised to marry him only if I was the last old-lady Norvelter. But by the time he sneaked back into town Mrs. Custard had returned, so I was no longer the last old lady. Huffer caught wind of Spizz hiding in the Community Center and he poisoned Mrs. Custard dressed as Spizz, who'd already confessed to the other crimes.

"Well, naturally, when she died I thought Spizz had killed her so I'd once again be the last old-lady Norvelter. That just really made me furious because I felt like a fool, like I had let Mrs. Roosevelt down because it was my fault Mrs. Custard was killed. And then when Spizz fled I wanted to go after him and put him six feet under. I knew he was going to Florida where he'd bought a hideout in the Everglades, but I couldn't get to Florida on my own, so I made up the part about my sister dying so your mother would allow you to help me get here, and it worked. Then I invited Huffer down to make the funeral look legit."

"Do you mean that all your hollering about killing the white whale was an act?"

"Not all of it," she said with a little fire in her voice. "In the beginning I made an oath I'd do him in. When that detective almost captured him in D.C. I fired my gun on purpose. I wanted to shoot Spizz myself. But once I was sure Spizz was telling the truth and that Huffer was the real killer, I wasn't as angry as I appeared. Honestly, I'm great with a harpoon and I should have winged him at Rugby just for the heck of it. And then when he was in the Amphicar and you pulled up next to him, I could have speared him right through the gills, but I missed on purpose."

"How did I not see all of that going on?" I said. It was mind-boggling that I never figured out what she was up to. "It's so obvious now."

"Remember the Proclamation Line historic marker you didn't see," she said. "Remember I told you that you missed it because you only see what you already know? Well, start looking for what you don't know. Tick-tock," she said, clucking her tongue.

"But why Spizz?" I asked.

"I've got more wrinkles on my face than a wad of tinfoil, and he's the only guy who would kiss an old lady like me. Sometimes love has the upper hand over a harpoon," she said with a smile. "And I'm glad it does, because I told you I wanted some love before the world blows up."

"You sure had me fooled," I said. "Was all the history real?"

"I could lie about Spizz," she said, "but I'd never lie about history. That is a crime!"

"Hang on," Dad called out. "We're going down."

We landed hard on a crusty old tarmac and bounced abruptly to a stop. Dad cut the engine, and once the prop stopped he stepped out on his side, and then helped guide Miss Volker down from the back. I jumped out on my side. I looked around. We were in the middle of the Everglades.

"I camp out here," Dad explained. "It's an old Army Air Corps strip and free parking for the plane while I look for work."

Spizz must have seen us land, and now that our engine stopped he drove out into the open and hit the horn on his Amphicar to give her a signal.

"I can't stay and talk," she said. "We have to get going—he's afraid the law is going to catch up to him."

"But he's no longer a wanted man," I said. "Aren't you going to tell him about Huffer?"

"I'm certainly *not* going to tell him," she said sneakily. "I still want him to think he's my Clyde and I'm his Bonnie."

"Really?"

"You know how he is," she said. "He'll be a much better boyfriend if he thinks I can call the cops on him and have him arrested."

"And I know how you are," I replied. "You love being in charge."

"I don't call myself Mrs. Captain Ahab for nothing," she replied.

I just had one more thing to say. I looked up at her and I knew I was going to cry. "This is the end of *our* history, isn't it?"

"Yes," she said. "But we *made* history together. Never forget that!"

How could I? "Do you need help to the car?" I asked, eager to lend a hand one last time.

"Nope," she said. "That's why I have the white whale. Your job ends here, now wish me luck."

I reached up to give her a kiss and felt the handbag on her arm. "I wish you would give me that pistol," I said. "That has been nothing but trouble."

"We need it for gators," she replied as Spizz's horn honked again. "And *other* pests." She jerked her head toward him.

"After I turn in the obit for Eleanor, do you want me to write your fake obituary?" I asked.

"Give me a week," she said. "Or a day, or maybe just an hour—or a few minutes." Then she turned, and with some spring still left in her step she walked on down to the Amphicar. Spizz swung open the door for her and guided her in.

He turned and waved. "Bye, Gantos boy," he hollered.

"Bye, white whale," I hollered back.

Then he put the Amphicar in gear and as he drove into the water the little cake-mixer propellers in the rear began to spin, and in a few minutes they had motored across the water and past a hammock of trees and around a bend and out of sight.

Dad came over to tell me to get a move on. I gave them one more fancy wave goodbye, like the starter at a horse race shouting "Go!" And that's when I heard the gunshot.

"Oh cheeze!" I cried out, and reached for my nose. "The bullet of history has been fired."

"What are you talking about?" Dad asked.

"She wrote in Mrs. Custard's obit," I explained, "that history would be made when the bullet finds its target. And now maybe it has."

"Well," Dad surmised, "one way or the other she got her man."

"Dead *or* alive," I added. "We'll never know. Sometimes history is a mystery."

"If I were you, I'd start writing an obit for Spizz." He turned and walked toward the J-3.

"That's a fact," I said. "Now let's go home."

"I have news for you. You're already there," he replied. "Your mom is flying in from Pittsburgh tomorrow, and I've rented a house in South Miami and start a new job this week."

"Really?"

"Look around you and say hello to paradise," he announced with his arms wide open.

I looked around and an alligator was crawling across the broken airstrip. It opened its powerful jaws and nosed up to the tire on the J-3 and snapped down on it.

"Is that the paradise welcoming committee?" I asked.

Just then the tire popped and the plane tilted to one side.

As Miss Volker always said, *"There's nothing but trouble in paradise."*

Jack Gantos was born in Norvelt, Pennsylvania, and has spent time living in Barbados and South Florida. He has written books for readers of all ages, including the acclaimed *Joey Pigza Swallowed the Key* and its sequels, the teenage novel *Desire Lines*, and the youthful memoire *Hole in My Life*.

His latest works are *Dead End in Norvelt* and *From Norvelt to Nowhere*, a pair of semi-autobiographical novels about the importance of history and reading, the first of which won the prestigious Newbery Medal in 2012. He lives with his wife and daughter in Boston, Massachusetts.